A TURN KEY JOB AND OTHER STORIES

Unsolicited Press
Portland, Oregon
www.unsolicitedpress.com
orders@unsolicitedpress.com
619-354-8005

Cover Design: Kathryn Gerhardt
Editor: S.R. Stewart

ISBN: 978-1-956692-47-1

A TURN KEY JOB
AND OTHER
STORIES

SUSAN PEPPER ROBBINS

Table of Contents

A Turn Key Job 7

I Know You 18

Like Debbie Reynolds 27

The Amusement Park 44

Good Afternoon, Mrs. Herndon 65

Risk Management 82

Honest Money 88

Irene's Five Year Plan 96

A Breath Away 101

Wyoming 113

What Matters 123

The Dodge and the Pontiac 133

Cremation Society 136

A Big Deal 141

Left-Over Vistas 152

White Women at Parties 161

Sabastian 171

Picking Up the Dead 189

A Turn Key Job

By May, the doors and windows are swollen and mildewed. The doors won't shut and the windows won't open. Turning on the central AC shrinks them back into their frames, but the electric bill shoots up. The commodes and refrigerator sweat avocado colored drops. Although the house is five months old, it may as well be an eighteenth-century home with all its problems.

Joyce and Ryland bear their new lives gracefully as if they had been inflicted on them and they are being cheerful and brave in the face of the storms they themselves have stirred up. Naturally, they don't feel that these storms blew up from the open seas of their personalities. In fact, they each believe greatly in the rolling calms of their beings. The storms came from meteorological conditions they simply had to react to. They are happy the storms are over and they have come through to their new house.

Joyce and Ryland don't look like home wreckers. She is stringy with gray eyes and the open and ready smile of a counselor. She is guiltless because she thinks guilt is old-fashioned and wasteful. The ability to follow her own advice—to avoid a waste of spirit—is her major talent as a counselor: she practices what she preaches to her clients. She is so organized she could have been president of General Motors, her mother always said in disappointment as she saw her daughter headed toward a degree in psychology. Now she says ruefully that Joyce will need those skills to run her new family of six.

Ryland is a shaggy, loud man who allows himself to be loved. Joyce knows from her training and her first marriage how rare a bird she's caught.

They are both forty-three and feel uneasy to be so in love with each other. They urge time to pass, unlike most people entering their forties, so that they will have been together longer and will have their own history when they are old, which will be in twenty years they say, surprised. They want a whole lifetime, their oceans, held in the twenty years they have taken away from their first husband and wife.

Time flies is not a truism for them; they wish it would, leaving them with a history of birthdays, trips, and "when's. "Now they are as new and exposed to their families and friends as the wave of red dirt the bulldozer left around their house like a sea wall against the woods and new houses going up.

The husband and wife they have left for each other are more attractive than they are. It is unflattering the way people are shocked by the re-grouping as if happiness and passion are reserved for the beautiful, and it is obvious that the house and marriage violate their friends' ideas about them and their shock is unsettling. It is irritating that even they feel miscast and misplaced in this dream house after friends visit them.

After a supper party, Joyce is upset and forced to see herself in a new way. It comes to her that her personality is porous and she feels anger sluicing through her. She always has thought of herself as a live-and-let-live person, but after Nell, their guest, had gone to bed, Ryland points out to her that she had "attacked" Nell for the way her girls have turned out.

Nell is taking a break from her Richard; now her hair floats in white curls around her face but is dark in the back like it was when she was younger.

"You're mad because she's on a vacation and you have these four kids of ours to handle. She's free—for a while—and you, poor you, will never be. "Ryland is trying to mock her into helplessness which often makes them laugh at themselves.

"You mean I went too far asking why Lillie and Clara never came home?"

"No, more than that. It should be clear to us, and I mean you, that she and Richard have grown children who have their own lives."

"Well, I get tired of things being off limits. We sure are raw meat for everyone."

Joyce is skillful at turning all subjects back to them and their situation. They need to tell their story over and over to give it the weight and history it lacks.

They are sitting in the kitchen recalling their first real phone call, their miserable time before their move outs, their ritual custody fights, and are beginning to feel better when Nell walks in, her white curls stuck to her face and her green scrub suit pajamas stuck to her in damp patches.

"Why do you seal your windows shut? Are you afraid I can't take a weekend with you and your orphanage?"

"We don't," they protest as Nell shakes her head at how far gone they are.

"You need a vacation," she laughs, "already. "She elaborately leads them by the hand to the guest room that is so warm the thermal windows are perspiring. "You are slipping," she says to Joyce who is trying to raise the windows. She remembers airing out the room right after Nell had called to say she was coming for the weekend, she didn't mention Richard. Joyce remembers the windows rushing up their aluminum runners.

"It's all right. You've been through some changes lately. I've got some squirtum stuff out in the car that would free Houdini. "Nell, like Joyce, uses the black phrases. One of her students writes about the Ugandan tribes "going through some changes."

Joyce answers, saying, "But here we be." Ryland fixes the windows with Nell's spray. The stuck windows have told the three of them more than they want to know about the changes in Joyce and Ryland's life.

Joyce works at the welfare office called the Human Services Agency and likes the shorthand of black English. Her secretary, Barbra Faison, is African-American. She is shocked but happy with the events in Joyce's life. In a way, Barbra understands Joyce's situation better than anyone. First, she wants to understand and puts out the effort. Second, as she has often told Joyce, she is black but not black. She is "of African heritage," and she has named her children names that sound African to her like Kalunda and Ateisha, but she is not black in the sense that many black people and white people like Joyce have tried to make her be.

She hates American soul food and music with their flavor of slavery and poverty. She is an Ibo, tall and above the street people and teenaged mothers who come in the office—not above them spiritually, she says, but in her dreams and ways. She has her G. E. D. and is working on a certificate in word processing. Her children are in the Talented and Gifted programs at school.

Until Barbra got her new asymmetrical haircut, she wore jerry curls. She likes high fashion and says that blacks have more sense of fashion than anyone. She wants to redo Joyce and brings her the white make-up she wins as bonuses for being made up in department stores at demonstrations. The packets are always for white people, she laughs. She makes fun of Joyce's faded denim and wrinkled linen look and tells her that unless it has Calvin Klein's name on it, it can't be wrinkled. Barbra's clothes are what Joyce always thought were worn to cocktail parties, high sandals, loose silk skirts and nubby tops. She is beginning to see how clothes can cheer a place up. Barbra sits at her desk like a thrown silk scarf. The clients appreciate the magenta and purple and ivory effect. Her lipstick and earrings match.

Like Barbra's Ibos, Joyce feels like her history with Ryland's has been violently interrupted. They are in a primitive, oral history period. She also feels jejune to appropriate Barbra's views for herself, but Barbra's generosity with them is tempting. "I been there too," is the most comforting thing Joyce has heard. It sounds like the key turning in the lock of their house.

Their home was a turn key house which means the contractor did everything, subbing out the wiring, septic tank, painting and bookcases. All Joyce and Ryland did was choose the avocado and earth tones, laughing at themselves for being so retro-trendy but still hoping for a calming, phlegmatic influence.

At night, the tree frogs sound like Barbra's keyboard—two spaces and a shift, two spaces and a shift. The house is on a four-acre plot in a new subdivision that is still country and raw. Space was a priority for their kids, two each. The house, so far, seems to please all four children who needed the diversion of building the house after the explosion of divorces which brought the six of them together at Tick Terrace as Ryland calls it. Each kid has his acre, theoretically.

Marriage had been put off until the house was ready for the big move and Joyce was exhausted by the makeshift domesticity, both old-fashioned and artificial, and the contrived high spirits it took to hide first, the adultery (Joyce and Ryland use antique expressions to lighten things up), and then, the affair that followed.

Washing and cooking for four children, keeping her own professional life going at the agency, and being in love had been too much for her. Eating junk food with the kids helped and drinking wine watching television cushioned her spirit at home and Barbra lifted her spirit at work.

She wishes she were a modern woman in every way, a runner or aerobics dancer, so that she would have the stamina she needs. Her modernity is targeted, as she says in her reports at the agency, on things marital. She plants tomatoes in the red wave of dirt around the house for the same reason she eats chips and watches junk—quietness descends.

Four children under eight, one hyperactive and one with Attention Disorder Syndrome, add to the forbidden riches of love. Also to the comedy, Joyce thinks defensively as she tries to make a breakfast that is downright motel in appeal. Ryland's Heather and Rylie have lived in motels almost as much as they have in the condo their parents had. They like the food they pick at to be served with flair.

As Joyce slides the knife in banked curves around each grapefruit half, she knows she is not getting the sections cut into spoon sizes. She puts a strawberry in the center of each one over the cores that she has left uncut to be worried with the dull-nosed cereal spoons.

She can't help but think of her mother's deft knack with grapefruit and her grandmother's silver-toothed spoons that have been lost in some of her recent "upsets" her mother calls them. Ryland appreciates her efforts at stabilizing his children and tempting their ruined appetites.

She guesses he considers it a compliment to her children, Iris and Eric, or to her as a mother, the fact that they eat whatever she fixes and will wring the juice out of grapefruit with adult intensity and care. She thinks there may be more to it than that. They gobble because they're not sure what is happening next. Iris is getting plumper and more golden every week. Eric is hyperactive so the food he wolfs down is burned up immediately.

They treat Ryland with a courtesy they use with no one else. He says don't knock it, and after the filthy insouciance of Heather, Joyce agrees. To them, he seems like a muzzled and staked bear, powerful but safe for the time being. They circle him, sticking out their hands. Iris makes him sandwiches and holds them over to him out of the reach of his swipe. Eric hops around him, doing Kung Fu kicks.

Heather and Rylie don't see him as a great Elizabethan street bear; he's a nerd who couldn't take the electrical shocks of living with their mother. They would have been happy, happier, to stay in the condo, opening cans of ravioli and listening to recorded messages telling them where Win, their mother, was and when she'd be back. They will have a hard time, like their new stepmother Joyce, making the adjustment to the wholesomeness, space, woods, and people.

"This is your dream house?" Nell had asked when she came, with some wonder in her voice as she looked up the two-story walls of books in the chalet room.

On four acres, draperies and curtains aren't needed so the sun shines in "without quarter," Ryland says, and has already blistered the polyurethane finish on the random width pine floors. They wonder what they will look like by August.

"Can't you tell?" the new couple had laughed to Nell. "Tells you everything about us and more than you wanted to know."

In the winter, the smoke from the wood stove had softened the bright white ceilings, making plumed shadows and fossils. They tried to read them like clouds when they lay on the new orange and navy blue rug looking up. In May, the six of them lie in the chalet room, being a family, staring at the ceiling, but without a fire to stoke. They miss the smoke swirling out the stove door when it is opened.

It's not the same. Nell's visit and the sealed window marked the end of their first phase in the house, the honeymoon. Now they are skirting the summer, the thin isthmuses of mildew connecting the house to the heats and damps to come. But at least, Joyce thinks, like Rylie has taught her to, we have the beginnings of a family life, a now and then. "*Ubi sunts* are supposed to last longer than five months," Ryland says.

"It's what is given, my pet, be smug, try complacency, you'll like it," Joyce answers, trying for her old quaint mockeries.

The brown rice was an uneven success for supper. Iris and Ryland enjoyed it. Eric and Rylie made tunnels and clover leafs with theirs. It takes three hours to get all four of them asleep.

"It's good we're married. I'd hate to be having an affair this way. No sex in marriage is more respectable and acceptable than with lovers. Joyce still has to pack lunches and lay out gym clothes, scout uniforms and regular stuff."

Homework is a lost art, but they promise themselves that next fall they'll get it together and structure things. It's after eleven when the three dogs are fed, things are more or less ready for tomorrow, and the house is more or less quiet. From the bedrooms upstairs that open into the upper air of the chalet, Joyce can hear the snorting and belching contests begin. These are the two sets of peace treaties, and being divided against each other, the girls in one room, the boys in the other, they are beginning to tolerate each other.

"Work toward toleration, not friendship," the family counselor had told them. "Keep your expectations minimal."

It was hard to get them up that high, Ryland said, shaking his head in a way Joyce hoped wouldn't become a habit.

Ryland is sick of the experts they've been through in the last year—the marriage counselors, lawyers, doctors, teachers (Eric is failing the first grade and has been since October. Ryland is sure the teacher labeled him "Broken Home" and decided then to hold him back), reading specialists and contractors. Even Rylie's Kung Fu instructor condescends in a professional way.

Rylie yells to his sister through the open doors, "At least, let's pretember we used to have funner times at night."

Heather yells back, "Shut-up, dum-dum. 'Pretember' is Rylie's amalgam of remember and pretend.

"Proustian," Ryland says, "in its implications."

Only it's not a mother's kiss he's trying to conjure up. He never had over a dozen. He's remembering the all-night horror movies they used to watch on cable and it seems now to him that it was fun—that's the pretend part. He was frozen stiff. That was his fun.

"Maybe more fun than looking at a smoky ceiling."

"Yeah, we're about as slow as they go." They laugh. This is love they say, maybe not true love, but it'll do. They make separate plans as they fall asleep to check the windows in the upper level of the chalet room near the smoke-scarred ceiling. Fresh air kills mildew.

Joyce, the more high-strung of the sleepers, also promises herself to sin only in the smallest ways against the children, like throwing away stray Legos and parts of toys.

16

In this way, she begins, as she would say to Barbra, to be what she is, an Ibo, by adoption into the tribe, above the situation, looking at the ceiling for signs of smoke and mildew. Maybe mildew and smoke will age the house quicker, wrenching it away from its youth as the children have been.

She plans to go in the woods tomorrow and find some moss and ferns to transplant between her tomato plants. With such high, modern feelings, she follows her new family into sleep where she hopes they wait for her.

I Know You

"I know you. That's the way I am. Always had the gift. I know people by their faces, and I can look at you and see that we are deep. Into each other, I mean. Excuse my shit, I mean, French, but I can see you, not through you, but see the you that you really are. You know what I'm saying. Friends. True Friends. That's us. Somewhere we have been best friends. It may be hard for you to take in right now. Somehow, I don't know how, but I do have this power or maybe it's a talent, but the fact is, I do know you. Somehow. Some Place. You think we are strangers but we are not. For damn sure. My family is from around here, not from right here in Charlottesville, but out in the country, so maybe somehow, I have seen you, and I know you in the regular way, I mean at a store in the mall, but I'm talking about knowing you in another way. Even though I grew up in New York."

"Yes, I see you thinking that I must be one of those black children sent back down South to live with a relative, only I was what you would call a contrarian. I was sent up North, not back down here to the south like a regular black baby whose mama brought her or sent her back home to her grannie. That's what you're thinking. Because you are a white person who grew up around here and never got sent nowhere, we might say. Or to put it in a more insulting way, a racist way from my point of view, you ain't never been anywhere much. I can tell that from overhearing you talk a few minutes ago. And I would know anyway from other little signs, not that I mean to insult you though I am afraid I have already. If I meant to, my friend, I would have. Believe me on that. I know you never lived in New York, not that that matters. But make no mistake, I know you."

"Even with all your little faults, you still are a beautiful person who feels what the other person is feeling, even a person who seems to be a stranger like me. A person you think you have never seen. And you can go the extra mile and what is even better, you want to. There aren't many people like that in this world, this terrible old world, I don't have to tell you. I can tell who you are, I mean who you really are in your soul."

As the black woman talked to her, Adeline had been handed a green bean and walnut salad—the beans were almost raw and the walnuts had been soaking in oil for too long. Then the woman sat down close to her in the gas station/café, closer than an old friend would, but since Adeline and the woman were both swirling glasses of wine, "a nice summer wine," expertly poured by the young man behind the counter, they looked something like old friends. He had offered both women a tray of little blocks of soft cheeses for them to spear on the toothpicks he gestured toward on the counter. The black woman swished the wine around in her mouth expertly, unlike Adeline who drank hers down as if she were at home drinking the cheap grocery store wine she and Gerald bought. He had started drinking it too at night with her. Not a good sign. Adeline knew it was dangerous to move from one glass to two. A gateway to worse things. From watching television, even good programs like "The Wire" or "Bleak House" they were moving to drinking wine and falling asleep half-way through the stories, sometimes in the news from Iraq.

Adeline was not a beautiful person, but it was great to be told that she was. As if she were a new version of Lana Turner at a drug store counter sipping a milkshake, and not a latter day Night Hawker, a failed somebody. She did often go the extra mile but ruined it by wanting extra credit for the trip, so it wasn't really so extra. Because she knew many bad things about herself, it was very nice to hear this crazy black woman say nice things with such authority, even a demented one. At last, here in this upscale gas station that had a lunch counter and wine tasting, Adeline had been understood and appreciated. This was one of the small miracles she had heard about. She was smelling the roses for once.

Internet gambling could be replaced with other addictive behaviors—credit card debt, for instance—Gerald's doctor had warned them that there were many, many ways to commit suicide. The three of them had smiled knowingly in the doctor's office during one of their three-way sessions. Gerald's doctor like this crazy woman knew Gerald, though they had just met him three months ago.

Adeline and Gerald were on their way home from a writers' festival in Charlottesville, a short story session that afternoon. There were only a few people there, all women except for Gerald and two other men. Maybe twenty people, tops. The one younger woman there, about forty, looked embarrassed and left early. The writers, three men, who read their stories were in their fifties, and successful in their tenured posts at colleges. Most of the festival crowd had gone to the sessions with stars like Earl Hamner or the policeman-turned-writer, George Pelacanos, on how to write what the media would buy. That was the other session Adeline and Gerald had gone to, where they had learned what Gerald already knew—that it was all hopeless—that there was no way to write what the media wanted because what the media really wanted the writer to know how to do was package the writing into hits, know how to approach the networks and sell the product.

It was clear that no one wanted short stories except, funny enough, other writers of stories, the short story panelists said, "a mystery, how they—they meant themselves and the few there who had come to the panel—were addicted to them." They were editors for little magazines, famous ones, and said they got five to seven thousand submissions a year, but published only twelve stories a year, and of those twelve, three were each other's stories. At least they were honest about the impossibilities. This was the first writing conference that Adeline had ever been to when the brutal facts were talked about so plainly. The panelists were the haves talking to the have nots, as Adeline's long ago seventh grade teacher had explained the world. This explanation of the great divide in humanity made things clear. It never failed to clarify things for Adeline in its bitter wisdom.

On the way home as they drove by the banks of bright yellow forsythia not quite hiding the trash thrown from cars, Gerald had seen the gas station that advertised a wine tasting in its Café. Typical of the twenty-first century Charlottesville—a pale gray building, discreet gas pumps and an area for wine, cheese, and "light fare." They had lived in this neighborhood as graduate students thirty years ago. Shocking the way time had flown, but there in the gas station, time hovered, as if it had nothing better to do than hang out with them, mixing up the past and present. Back then during their graduate school folly, they had frantic lives of being in love, of studying, and finally, failing to make impressions on the famous professors. Where they had lived, this area across town from the university had been called Cow Pasture. Now it went by a new name, Belview, gentrified with boutiques and places like this café/gas station managed by a kid who was an expert in wines. He probably spoke Farsi and was writing a dissertation on Coleridge. Some things never changed in Charlottesville.

Gas was three dollars and ten cents a gallon, but to soften that, there were taped signs on the pumps saying "Sorry, We Are Out of Gas Temporarily, But Come in for Our Wine Tasting." The green bean salad was four dollars (there were eleven beans and eight halves of English walnuts) and Gerald's "fried" chicken (baked in the wrong, too sweet cornmeal) was five ninety-five.

Adeline and Gerald now thought about the money they spent, not that their thinking saved any of it for them, but at least they thought about their bad habits, like this one of buying supper in a gas station tarted up as a café when they were almost at home and could fix something better from the huge supplies of vegetables and meats they bought at Sam's every two weeks in excursions to the city, combining their shopping with seeing Gerald's doctor. Often the broccoli which could last five weeks, went bad, slimy, but the big bag of carrots lasted forever, and always tasted the same, hard and orange, like cardboard soaked in orangeade.

The black woman was now launching into her story of widowhood at twenty-one after five years of marriage. She was explaining her New York accent, her career as a waitress that had made her so good at knowing, "we might call it reading" people. She directed her remarks to the empty tables around Adeline, as if she had an overflow crowd. It was like the short story session in small. She stood up to walk the few steps over to the wine counter off to the side of Adeline, for her second plastic cup of the wine. This time she said she would like one a little sweeter, but before she took a step, she carefully put the metal cap back on the quart-sized beer she had in a paper bag.

The young manager politely told her that state law would not permit him to give her another taste of the wine, that she had had several tastes already, and that he was very sorry, and was happy that she had enjoyed the summer wines, the drier ones. She politely told the young man that he had a very nice way with different kinds of people and that she could tell he had a beautiful soul, and that he would go far in his life, that she could tell, that she knew him, that she had this gift for knowing people from their faces. She had always been able to spot good people. Here, she looked kindly at Adeline and Gerald who had been losing their hold on themselves as good people for some time.

Adeline could see the back of the woman's jeans were damp, darker than the pale denim of the legs when she flicked back her plastic raincoat. There was the urine smell of the nursing home in the small area of the café made sharper by the dry weather. It hadn't rained for weeks.

The woman sat back down and began making gargling noises, clearing her throat and staring at Adeline who was avoiding by instinct any eye contact, but then the woman addressed her directly from two feet away, "I am speaking to you and would appreciate your acknowledging me. I am a human being too, you know. I have been to the god damned writing festival myself, which is where I can tell you have been."

"Would you have a twenty that I could borrow? I need twenty to finish up my rent, and I am a little short. I am a writer, like you are yourself, and so I know that you know what a twenty coming out of the blue means to a person. I will go home now after seeing the people I know, like you and your man, and write down what I saw. I'm no Mark Twain, but I do love him. I love you too. But Earl Hamner was great today. I didn't see you there at his session, but I went up to talk to him, and I can tell you, he was great. If I missed you there, if you really were there, you know that what I'm saying to you now is the truth. Earl Hamner who wrote all that jive about white hill people being so good hearted is a good man. I am here to tell you."

At this point, the woman stood up, bent, her long hair hanging from under a baseball cap, her rain coat glistening as if she had been in a nice rain. She adjusted her shoulders elegantly. She was saying again to the air around Adeline and Gerald's table that she guessed she would go home now, and ask her landlord to stand by her for another day when she would get a check, she was expecting one on Tuesday or certainly on Wednesday. She would write about them—she had asked Gerald and Adeline from the cash register for ninety-seven cents to finish up her bill and the twenty as a loan—yes, she would write about Adeline, the beautiful person she was talking to now, put her in her journal along with all of the good people she knew. Not all of them could help her, as Adeline could, but those who could, did help her. Some day, people would know how much she had been helped by strangers, not that she thought of them as strangers now after she had had wine together with them in the cafe after the writers' festival.

Adeline felt herself slip the twenty-dollar bill, the one she always kept zipped in the side pocket of her purse into the woman's hand. She felt that she was in a trance of some kind though she often felt like she and Gerald were living in another dimension. It would have made more sense to her then and later if the woman had had a knife or a gun or at least pretended to have one in the paper bag with the beer. But all the woman, homeless looking, had done was talk kindly to her, maybe the way Gerald's doctor talked to him.

Then the woman left the café. She did not acknowledge the money from Adeline.

"It's so sad," Adeline said to the young wine pourer, giving him permission to say back to her, "It is so sad." She needed to cover up what she had done with some words about the general condition of humanity. The young man was familiar with this need in customers. He shook his head sadly over the world with Adeline, probably saying a few lines of ancient Persian poetry to himself.

She turned to look at Gerald and asked if he had paid for the bottle of wine that she had told the young man they would buy when he had given his description of the kinds of evenings it was perfect for. Gerald said that he had already paid for it. Had he stepped out and put the bottle in the car when Adeline had gone to the bathroom? No, he hadn't, he said, and then he added in his witty way, "Not that I recall. Did you put it in the car?" No, she shook her head.

"Do you have the receipt?" Adeline said this to keep the young manager from having to ask Gerald if he had it. No, Gerald didn't have it, but the young man at the cash register would know, would remember that Gerald had paid for the bottle of wine, just a few minutes ago, maybe ten, and when Gerald looked across the small café, the young man smiled in confirmation: yes, the bottle of wine had been paid for. Definitely.

Then the young man began turning one hand over and shrugging with one shoulder, knowing before Adeline and Gerald knew, what must have happened. Then he shrugged both shoulders, coordinating the move with now two turned-over hands.

"Maybe it isn't sad," he said. "For her, anyway. It's a little sad for me because I'll have to make it up in the inventory and add a bottle from the wine shop on the mall, but I have to give it to her, she got me this time." It was clear that he admired the woman. Adeline found herself agreeing.

Gerald offered, insisted, on paying for the bottle of wine again, but the young man waved the offer away, saying "Forget it, not a problem. I'm cool. My company expects this to happen and expects me to cover it. They say they know a good man when they hire one. All in a day's work."

Like Debbie Reynolds

I got marriage out of my blood before I was thirty. It took two husbands, and since then—for many years now—like Debbie Reynolds, I have not dated. Unlike my friend Abby who's stuck with that lone wolf Clark.

Recently, Ms. Reynolds was interviewed on *20/20* or maybe it was *Dateline*. She said the dating part of her life was over. Everyone watching in America could feel what she was feeling as she talked about Eddie Fisher and men in general. Her decision to give up men was a great, but necessary loss not only to men, but to herself, and it was a shame.

"It's sad," she smiled in a very maturely pretty way. "But, it's a fact."

But, it's not over for my sisters by a long shot. Martha and Harriet are just getting started with their love lives in their fifth and sixth decades. They have not reached the higher ground that Debbie and I have achieved.

For the record, my first husband, Bill, turned out to be a drunk, a quiet one with manners from Europe, and as serious as the medieval scholar he should have been. But, circumstances mixed with alcohol changed his plan for studying Aquinas, and he worked his short life in real estate, finding houses that had not yet been put on the historical register but were eligible because no one had bought them up from the old families with enough money left to ruin or improve them with swimming pools and decks, garages and barns for their children's horses.

William Alexander Stone was dead within a year of our divorce, the summer of '73, when Watergate was on television. It turned out that Bill had been politely waiting for me to leave to begin to drink seriously, and when I did finally have sense enough to leave, I flung his grandmother's ring down the stairs of the old house, the one we were living/camping in until he could find the right young couple to see it as a bargain and treasure.

Mansion is too strong a word. It had twelve rooms and double-decker porches that looked down on a narrow river. My violence shocked him, but convinced him, that the marriage was over. He probably thought I was going to run out to the hundred-year-old shed and get an axe and try to murder him as he sat by the long window in what was once the library though the books were in stacks on the floor because the walnut shelves had been stolen.

His great-great-great aunt had come to the house as a bride and left twelve years later as an impecunious widow in 1863 when she walked away, half-crazy with three small children. Bill's grandmother was the middle girl in that straggling band of four who hid in the woods from both Confederate and Yankee soldiers. She had been taken in as an orphan by her mother's sister when her parents died with tuberculosis. The house had been abandoned, but never sold, and hardly ever seriously lived in, that is, with generations succeeding each other. Instead, it acted as a way station. Some desperate cousins had "sought refuge" there during the Depression. They had raised chickens in one of the front rooms where we found the chicken wire still up, strung across the room to make a corner of it a coop.

Bill was able to prove that he owned the house, being the only heir left. This was a good thing, because we did not own anything else or have any other place to live.

This big ramshackle house was called "Evening Star" after the cottage in Wordsworth's poem, Bill said, and added that it suited a love such as ours, and I went along with his view of us until the ring-flinging incident. We decided after two years of camping there with a hotplate rigged up to a transformer that it should be sold to the new people who said that they would do justice to the house, "justice" they kept repeating, even if they would not promise not to put in central air or add a deck.

"Evening Star" had a family of black snakes in one of the big front rooms. After my ring-flinging, Bill drank himself into a coma, thence into his grave, but before he did, he made sure I understood that I was in no way to blame for his drinking problem. I agreed.

My second husband's problem was money, big time. Thomas Whitt Sheridan. Again, I married a real estate man. Later, I could see this pattern in my life events—love of property/loss of property.

Sherry, as his closest friends called him, which meant everyone he knew, was like Bill Stone, a developer of country estates hidden in the piedmont, houses built in the early eighteenth century by younger no-good sons, wastrels and blackguards whose houses were still standing because of the good materials and cheap labor. The loss of slave labor was deeply regretted by many of Sherry's friends too pc to say so. What they would say was that they wanted some Mexicans to do the work Americans wouldn't.

Many of the houses Sherry acquired before he went belly up claimed kin to Monticello because of their Doric columns and metapes, and in fact, as he began his financial slide, people called him Mr. Monticello, remembering Mr. Jefferson's money troubles. Sherry's fall and the collapse of his company, made the newspapers, and got him disbarred, (he had "read law" he used to say, but never intended to practice), and ruined my credit rating. Friends said Sherry damn well almost went to jail, but then they added that if Sherry were ever locked up, basic things in the universe would have to change—the sun would come up in the west, backwards over Lynchburg, scrolling forward eastward over Richmond to the Atlantic, across Norfolk and Portsmouth, in the wrong lane on I-64, setting in the east, causing wrecks in the commuter traffic, blinding the drivers.

Unlike Bill, Sherry did his real estate developing cold sober. Unlike Bill, he was not movie-star handsome but in the ball park, and like movie stars seem, he was perfectly indifferent to his looks which increased his value to women. Most men will pause in front of a mirror and check a sleeve or tie, or glance in the rear-view mirror at their shave. Not my Sherry.

Fast cars, slow women, he said when he met me, and I fell for it. Bill had had no interest in cars. His van had over two hundred thousand on it, and Sherry had no interest in houses except as items to market. He would have died if he had had to spend a night in an old house. We lived five years in a cheapo Richmond townhouse apartment, but we went through a smoke gray jaguar, a Mercedes convertible and a beamer. We would drive them by turns to every restaurant and race (horse or car) within two hundred miles of Richmond. We belonged to all the clubs that accepted payment plans.

I see now that I thought that I was playing the old game of dichotomies with my husbands. Bill or Sherry. This was a game we used to play, racing across the living room of a townhouse in Richmond's Fan District, forcing people to choose one or the other, calling out ice cream or cake, hill or vale, you or me, fire or ice, dancer or dance, death or divorce. I thought that Bill and Sherry were opposites, but I was as wrong as Newt Gingrich was when he went up against the Clintons. No, Bill and Sherry were two peas in a pod, but I thought they were night and day.

The problem with being married to a drunk is that it blinds you to other problems. So when Sherry didn't drink, I thought I was home free because this present husband was sober. I don't think I had ever heard of anyone going bankrupt when I met Sherry. Money was "ever a problem," to paraphrase somebody, but not desperately one, and not one that called for legal action. I thought that it was a simple coincidence that Bill and Sherry were both in real estate, not understanding that real estate attracts suicides of all degrees.

Dichotomies' one rule was that you had to choose your answer without a word of discussion. We had played dichotomies in graduate school to relieve the strain of trying to find the "reading" or the "implied or ideal reader" to "unpack" a poem. Ocean or Mountains, we'd yell. Silk or

31

Linen. Yeats or Joyce. Achilles or Hector. We could get predictive. Suicide or AIDS.

I took my belated vow of chastity after Sherry fell apart and have kept it so far. I was at a dangerous age then, I realize, mid-thirties. Now in my fifties, I feel vulnerable again, not to men, but to the knife cut of loneliness.

Last year I hiked the Appalachian Trail, well, parts of it. This year who knows? I've asked for a leave of absence from teaching freshman comp and if I get it, I'll go to California and try to be a new person, or better yet, find a person, man or woman, who will roam the wide world, figuratively, with me. This is not to say that I am bi-sexual. I am no longer sexual, and I truly believe that there are many people like me and Debbie Reynolds, the Been Theres, Done Thats.

Martha, the older of my two sisters, is a soft-bosomed sixty-three, a virgin, I thought, when she married Charles Parker. Harriet, now fifty-six, is a runner who weighs less than she did at twenty-two. She's divorced from David, the father of her two grown children and involved with a man she has not told us about. She likes secrets and despises confessions. Secrets give resonance to ordinary life. She does not think that her love life is anyone's business but hers.

The way Harriet looks, stringy and modern, as well as her age—both the chronological one and the younger one in the mirror—is a fact which she enjoys holding over Martha's head, but not over mine because I don't count, don't register. I have big bones and no one ever thinks whether I am fat or thin, old or young, I am just there. Both Harriet and Martha know that I have taken the pledge—no sex, no men—so I don't matter in many ways. When I am not around, out doing my thing like hiking the Appalachian Trail last spring, it's fine with them. California will be a perfect way to deal with me. They'll say to each other in their Thursday night calls that Claudia's gone off somewhere again, knowing I'll come back before long.

All three of us sisters live outside of Richmond in the three surrounding Southside counties, one sister per. Harriet in Chesterfield, Martha in Powhatan and me, farther out, in Cumberland. Powhatan has malls so new the cows are still grazing around the edges of the parking lots, Chesterfield's are old enough to have closed down for revitalization.

"About your age," Harriet will say to Martha as the final description of a new person she's met. The seven-year difference between Harriet and Martha is a chasm to Harriet, one which widens every day in her favor. And as I have said, I don't count, so the three-year gap between Harriet and me does not matter.

Age gaps do not diminish as people move toward the grave or the sky, although many people think that they do. In fact, the difference between fifty-six and sixty-three is the difference between water and ice. To younger people, maybe it is true that all older people look the same, but to oldies, every year, every month counts. I have even heard senior citizens talk about a three-week age difference.

Last year when I was taking Martha for her successful radiation treatments, she announced that she would be getting married.

"Wonderful," I said. I am very careful with my sisters, not that they return the compliment. "Who's the lucky guy?"

"You don't know him."

How true, would have been carefully and presciently an appropriate answer and should have been what I said. What Harriet asked me when I reported this news that I was sure that she already knew, was "How old is he?" Of course, Harriet was mad that Martha had told me the big news first.

Harriet wants to know things first, wants information of any kind, especially any bulletins from the sexual universe as she calls it.

In September, on a Tuesday, the fourteenth, her radiation just finished two days ago, Martha married Charles Parker, who eight months later drowned in the bathtub. Not like Agamemnon, Martha said under her breath to Harriet and me. We both knew she was not being flippant, that she was really heart broken.

Under all the sister stuff, we do love each other, but we do have our go-arounds. Harriet discusses our sisterhoods at length with me and behind my back with Martha, and we do the same—Martha and I—we talk about Harriet. Part of the whole system is that Martha and Harriet seem worlds apart, from distant galaxies as my students say. As different as my husbands seemed to me.

"Keep things straight" I say, careful even when I am speaking to myself.

In fact, Charles Parker turned out to be Harriet's age, seven years younger than Martha. An unheard of thing, to us, if not to movie stars, but to us, remarkable. I thought that all men looked younger than they were, but Charles looked old, up by several rungs, the ladder of years. Martha and

Charles were married for eight months, twelve if you count the four months before the wedding when he lived with Martha and helped her finish the radiation treatments. I appreciated his help with the driving and dinners.

Martha teaches Greek and freshman composition at the local college and after she retires in two years, there will be no more Greek, even in translation, she says, at every opportunity, even inappropriate ones, like Charles's death, she uses her Greek, mentions it, and makes an allusion, even a ghastly one, like the one to Agamemnon's bathtub murder.

"Eureka," she says when she finds her glasses or a student's folder on her desk. "Thalassa" she calls out as we get near any body of water, or "Hoi Polloi" to the mall walkers. She assigns paper topics to her freshman writing classes that she hopes will attract some classics majors but the numbers are still down. "My Summer Initiations: Drinking and Sex: Ancient Love Practices."

Last year one of her students explained to her that at her age, she might not get what he was saying about sex or even drinking. Might not understand the hierarchy of sexual practices. Might not know what men feel or why they need to drink. He was eighteen and apologized for speaking for all men, but still, he was sure that she could not possibly know what men feel, especially about sex.

Charles Parker was an insurance broker, and an "independent scholar" he called himself. He had been hired to teach the humanities classes no one else would teach, filling in for professors on sabbaticals at Gannon, Martha's college. It suited him as a dilettante, a renaissance type who said he knew a little about most things.

Harriet called herself an "independent physician" after she heard what Charles had the nerve to call himself and started prescribing St. John's Wort, ginseng and noni juice. She said all of Charles' knowledge, self-styled, came from crossword puzzles where her own came from. She was trying to change herself with exercise and herbs. Her mind would follow the healthful changes in her soma. The mind could take care of itself if the body led the way. The mind could see or feel the wisdom of the body. Her organs would smile, and then her spirit would. I believe she once said something off the wall like that. Observation was therapy, entertainment, religion. Why read fiction with all that was spread out before us on the lawn of the world! Why indeed, she would laugh. And, she had the stories to back her up on the endless variety of minds and bodies at odds—friends who had married men in prisons who were slated to be executed for rape and murder. It really had happened to her friend Brenda. She married the death row confessed murderer and was paying for him to have a new set of lawyers.

But Harriet was a trooper and helped me put on the wedding for Martha and Charles, and we did it right as if Mart were a nineteen-year-old girl in 1957, and HarHar and I were her small town banker father and garden club mother. Small, Episcopalian, Southern. I soaked the ham for three days, sawed off the hock and let it simmer twelve hours in a pan so big it sat on two burners. I had it sliced so you could see the world through a slice, rosy and salty, if you held it up to the window. We invited the thirty people we still knew that did not have trouble driving. Had the tablecloths starched. Harriet polished the pieces of old silver we still had and the brass lamps and fenders.

Harriet and I talked as we got ready for the wedding. I went into what Harriet pointed out was victim whining or whinnying and we did have to laugh at me. It has not done me any good to be the baby in my family, not gotten me off any hooks with my sisters, and they bring up Bill and Sherry as if Bill were still alive and Sherry still driving me to the races. With Martha and Harriet as older sisters, there was no chance that I would be spoiled. I am their everything. They own me, their slave. This was my plea as the old hymn goes. Though spoiled, I am not allowed to complain, whine, even muse on my troubles. They are bored with my infantile problems before I open my mouth.

Martha was wrecked by the terrible accident. Charles had been reading in the tub, drinking scotch after his sleeping pill, had fallen asleep and then slipped down, more an Ophelia than Agamemnon. Mart said she was just getting used to being happy. Harriet and I were adjusting to her happiness too. Hearing stories about Charles' taking her on golf trips—she had never held a club before—their outings to the mountains or the ocean, their staying up all night together to read novels, made me pretend to be jealous and Harriet nauseous.

Mart had been sure that I was falling in love with the idea of them, the whole thing of their late romance and late-in-life marriage in spite of my chastity vow. Who could resist this Charles who had discovered Martha whom he called his Elgin Marbles, his Chapman's Homer, his peaks of Darien and the ocean. Harriet, looking at Mart and Charles' love gibberings, googamooga goo goo, wanted to vomit, but went for a longer run instead, but as I said, HarHar knocked herself out helping me throw the fancy-ancy wedding.

Charles Parker was the perfect man and his lies, well, they were perfect too. He was a man, wasn't he? Eight little months. Maybe eight months was all that the cover-up/marriage could sustain. Bad health, a drinking problem, two ex-wives and an angry girlfriend in a Cadillac convertible, will out.

Now, Charles' children, George and Pauline, are taking Martha to court for negligence, though they must know how happy their father was during those eight months. Charles never mentioned his blackouts to Martha or to his children, nor even the dizziness. His lies were the silent types. He never told Martha about the first wife, just about the second one, the mother of George and Pauline.

In their shock, their disbelief that Charles, their father, drowned in his new wife's bathtub George and Pauline could have had Martha charged with something worse than negligence. I try not to hint at criminal negligence, the "m" word even. Harriet holds back too.

But, Martha shakes her bracelets, two thin silver ones, and asks what am I talking about, what could I mean. How can I add to her torment? Martha ends conversations that are losing their points with a gesture, lifting her shoulders and weeping as if I were not there, my non-essential self, as she is murmuring about being alone and running out of steam. I am of no use, she makes clear with her tears and murmurs.

Useless, I turn to Harriet who takes a turn with Martha.

Harriet has her own set of circumstances. She refuses to admit, maybe to herself, that she lets Ellis Winters stay over at her apartment every weekend now. Joan and Owen, her children, say they will not speak to her if she continues to have Ellis for sleep-ins, stay-overs, though they speak plenty to me, about the situation. They want me to tell Harriet that adultery is dangerous, and perhaps still wrong.

"Let Harriet know, tell her that we know what's going on." Joan has seen Ellis Winters with his wife at Food of All Nations. Joan bets her life on Ellis Winters' still being married. We have not met Ellis Winters—how could we when he is a secret—but Joan knows what he looks like through one of her groups that she works with, either Literacy or Aids Awareness. When I try to hint at this fear of Joan's to Harriet, this sighting, she says her children are liars, especially Joan who is, according to Harriet, a genius at covering her tracks so that she, Joan, always looks good, right.

Like Martha, I do not have children, and so the violence and misery of the ways parents and children deal with each other—trying to outdo each other, egging each other on, reaching for throats, sinking short swords in up to the hilt—how they talk to or about each other still surprises. Harriet talks about Joan and Owen as if they were agents for Saddam or Milosevic, and though I should be used to it, I am not.

"She has no soul," Harriet says about Joan. "He can't wait to dance on my grave," about Owen. "Both of them are killers by instinct and training. They would embezzle from Jesus, his loaves and fishes, the widow's mite. "To see the three of them together is to see a study in cameo, carved profiles gently and mildly meditating on love and nature. They look alike, their beautiful profiles reflect the same gene pool, and their tastes and love of nature reflect it too."

"It's only Ellis Summers they want to steal," I say, using his name as if Harriet had told me her secret, all about the man she is dating, the man on the historical society board. I am trying to steer Harriet back to her role in her children's transferred violence and treachery. I am hoping she will get mad at the Summers children who are roughly the same ages as Joan and Owen if I can think of something they might say if they knew about their father's weekends with Harriet. Harriet just looks at me as if I were a foreign exchange student who would be returning to Tanzania in a day or two, so there is no need to correct my English. And, I have not been able to think of a set of plausible lies to explain how I know Ellis Summers' name and connection to Harriet.

Joan and Owen are as savage about Harriet, though nothing children can do or say sounds as terrible as what parents say about children. This is the end-all and be-all, the alpha and omega of what I have learned about children and parents from Harriet. Owen has said casually to me on the phone, "Mom twisted Joanie's and my lives into perversions of activity. She has paralyzed us from the ankles up." This from a young man who got the internship in internet marketing in London, won the full stipends, then got the entry level position at 67,500. I do manage to say to him that he's doing all right.

All of these accusations fly in triangles across their bi-weekly suppers taken in turn at each one's apartment or a restaurant to which I am invited as a U. N. peacekeeper, an observer in the former Yugoslavia. Joan thinks that as her mother's sister, as their aunt, I should know how far Harriet has failed them, her children, and to be fair, she adds, how far from the mark they, the children fall. My role? I am to exclaim over their failures and bind up their wounds, all victims, but behind each other's backs—no side must know that I am Flo Nightingale to the other side.

Maybe I do keep them from arming with a Beretta as they eat plates of spaghetti and Greek salads.

Now, I predict that Ellis Winters will be included in the weekly dinners, a rectangle of assaults. Owen and Joan will want him there for the kill, for the slow turning on the spit over the fire of raw personality. Can an adulterer have dinner with the grown children, Joan and Owen, or his mistress—that old word-- who has yet to admit that he spends nights with her, that she even knows him. We seem to have forgotten that this is the new millennium. We're trapped in 1957.

And who am I that I must do this shuttle diplomacy? I am Claudia, fifty-three, the two-husband baby of the family, the one with the advice never taken, but always demanded. I say to Martha when I meet her for lunch: "Get a lawyer to handle Charles' insane children," and "Don't retire until the college drags you out. Keep bribing the students to take your Greek 101. It's dying out, but don't speed it up. "To Harriet when she comes by for my rosemaried carrots and roasted leg of lamb," I say, "Get rid of Ellis, but first, admit that he is in your life, that he is married. He's not worth it. You look

41

like and are a fool. Listen to your children who are, God knows, terrifying, but they are not liars."

Then I go forward, outlining my plans to save my sisters: buy a grandfather clock kit, rent a house in the mountains. Rewire their houses whether they need it or not. I try to set a good example and have taken up herb gardening and sky diving myself. Joan and Owen like the news that I am jumping from planes because I am only an aunt. They are mild in their ridicule, not hatefully murderous as they would be about such news from their mother. They are kind to their Martha, their Marmar too, that is, they do their laughing behind her back. "Poor Martha-Lartha," they laugh. "Charles, drowned in the tub? Have you ever heard of a better way to go?"

I get us all together for lunch—a mistake—and to avoid the subjects of Charles' death and Ellis Summers' secret weekend life, we talk about David, Harriet's ex-husband, Joan and Owen's dad who left them before they started daycare—eight months for Owen and eighteen months for Joan.

Harriet will talk about David. He was a letter writer and she says she was the victim of his letter writing talents.

"His letters brought me back to him. Once from Cleveland, once just from Fayetteville. He'd send me twelve pagers detailing the anatomy of my spirit—no mention of my body which should have suggested a problem or the whole trouble, but I could not get enough of the letters. And then, he'd wait for me to come noodle-headed home. That would hold me until I left again."

Then she shocks us by saying "You may ask why letters when I'm the one who loves sex. Feel free. I went for the letters, I can't believe it myself, because I can't write, not like that, and anyone who does write good letters, has me in hand, by the throat, over a barrel, dead to rights, at the end of the barrel."

Of all stupid things, given who we are and what's happened, we are telling love stories over lunch. Martha, the new widow, tells Harriet that premature ejaculation can be treated to which Harriet says that she and David never discussed sex. Everything else but. Love, yes, sex, no. She and David talked about love over three-hour Indian dinners cooked with the help of the library staff who found the old books on curry and the British influence on the ancient preparations of curry. But then I would leave again.

Then Martha says, "I don't know what I would not forgive." Does she mean Charles' carelessness with his life that night in the bath? His lies about his health or his first wife? Is her forgiveness bottomless? That's the only thing she can mean.

Harriet's divorce from David came through the mail, civil, a matter of paperwork, like his love letters.

How are we to account for Joan and Owen? There were also miscarriages. These from such inadequate sex! "They just came like the leaves, not so many, thank God, but fell on me, not like leaves, but bricks."

Joan and Owen to their eternal credit die laughing.

This is our lunch.

The Amusement Park

Thomas has said that he is not going with them to see Dr. Thia, the new doctor, and hear him beat up on Jeffrey for playing video games the way the other doctor had. So what if Jeffrey plays all night and sleeps all day. Jeffrey is twenty-three and should do what he wants when he wants. Thomas does not mention that his older brother has been in trouble with the police, but the thought seems to cross his mind because he shrugs and uses Jeffrey's words—the games help Jeffrey "get by," they help him not feel "real wasted." Jeffrey didn't do anything wrong anyway. It was Chris and Tony who took the cd's from the Seven-Eleven. And, Tony'd wrecked the car. They were the drunk ones. Jeffrey wasn't even in the car.

Thomas is eleven and defends his brother to the death. This first visit to the new doctor is supposed to be a family visit, and so he has to go.

Nell's going too even though she isn't family. Two years ago, she and Richard rented an upstairs apartment from Darlene and Franklin Morris, the long-suffering grandparents of Jeffrey and Thomas, and now Nell feels like part of their family, especially of the Jeffrey story. She wants to be. It takes her mind off her own problems at home with Richard who is taking a break of two weeks from his job in Georgia.

In fact, it's Nell who's found the new doctor, this Dr. Thiagarajah, who wants to be called Dr. Thia, and who wants a family visit the first time he sees Jeffrey, and Nell is now family. The other doctor was also Indian or Pakistani. Dr. Patel had tried a version of tough love on Jeffrey but it failed, and so they are putting all their money on this new doctor that Nell has found.

Darlene is afraid that Thomas is headed in the same direction that Jeffrey has taken. Thomas can't/won't ride the school bus so his mom Paula drives him to school. He can't ride a bike or swim. What he can do is order popcorn shrimp at Appleby's and play video games. His favorite food is lobster; popcorn shrimp are a concession to whoever is treating him because shrimp are cheaper. His grades are good because of Darlene's help. But, so were Jeffrey's. Thomas is treated with great deference, the last chance in the family. He plays it for all it's worth. Nell could tell them what's going on with Thomas but she's lost her confidence in seeing what's what.

The morning of the afternoon appointment with Dr. Thia, Jeffrey had printed out forty pages of information from the internet for Thomas to use for his games. He tries to repay Thomas for his loyalty.

What can this Dr. Thia know about American young people? Nell imagines that his white coat will have a Nehru collar that his black hair does not touch. It turns out to be just as she imagined. He comes out from behind his desk into the circle of chairs where they all sit. Nell had been shocked that Thomas had been going with his brother to Dr. Patel, who had tried to outlaw video games for Jeffrey. She had thought it was a healthy sign that Thomas did not want to go to this new doctor. But Darlene told her that Dr. Thia had called her himself to say that he wanted as many of Jeffrey's family as were able to come to this first session. "The more the better. Supersize," he had said on the phone to Darlene. That's when he had asked that they all call him "Dr. Thia."

Darlene tells Nell that Dr. Thia charges more for a family visit. Nell offers to pay her part, a fifth, but Darlene says, no, today, Nell will be Dave, playing the part of Jeffrey's dad, taking his place. But if she is Dave, Nell says, she should pay, at least for this first family visit anyway, but she has only a twenty in her pocketbook which she gives to Jeffrey who takes it. Jeffrey is no longer covered by his dad's health insurance.

Nell knows many Jeffrey stories. Once he left his mom, dad and brother locked out of the house in the rain after he had crawled through the window to open the door. They were at the front door waiting for him. They had forgotten their keys, as Nell remembers the story, but when Jeffrey had gotten in through the window, he forgot about brother and parents, went to bed and fell asleep with them still knocking on the locked door. Paula, Dave and Thomas had finally gone over to Darlene's house to spend the night, afraid, Nell guesses, that Jeffrey was so angry that he was refusing to open the door for them. They never know exactly what his actions mean. But they try to make sense of what he does. Jeffrey may not know what he means either. What he says sometimes has a deep wit to it, Shakespearean almost. He told Nell that Tony, the guy who got drunk with Chris, had only one arm, but that he would not like Chris if he had two. Jeffrey had smiled when he said this, and Nell had understood it, for a minute anyway.

For the forty-five minutes with Dr. Thia, they will owe two hundred dollars, and with Nell's twenty, they could pay ninety upfront before they walked into the session. Darlene will send a check for the rest. It's humiliating Nell thinks to pay upfront for the treatment at the receptionist's window before they even meet this Dr. Thia, much less know if what he has to offer will work. Dr. Patel's tough love counseling sure hasn't worked. She doesn't know if he charged his patients before or after their counseling sessions, and she doesn't know if Jeffrey will keep her twenty or give it to his grandmother to help with the bill.

Richard Who? Nell thinks happily, refusing to remember that Richard cuts on the heat even though it's ninety degrees and dry. He's "chilled to the bone," he says. He tries to make sense of it, she thinks, when he laughs and says, that he's used to Georgia where it's tropical.

Jeffrey will drive them to Dr. Thia's but maybe not back home. His grandmother will have to drive. He's learned to say to them that treatment is exhausting. Maybe it is, or maybe Jeffrey uses that line to get out of things. It's thirty-seven miles down the interstate to Dr. Thia's office.

They try to use the time in the car as Dr. Thia in another phone call has asked Darlene to try to do on the trip to his office. He wants them to "wam up" she said he had said, in order to talk openly about Jeffrey's problems. They can get started before he meets them as a group at three o'clock. This is brutal advice, but Nell starts, feeling Darlene silently begging her to get them going.

Thomas had been upset, Darlene has told Nell, when Darlene had asked Dr. Patel if they should be worried about

Jeffrey and suicide. Darlene has reported on the two years' worth of visits to Dr. Patel to Nell. At that visit, the one Darlene calls "the suicide visit," when Thomas had been sitting on the floor because his dad had gone with them that time, and all the chairs were taken, Dr. Patel had said, of course, they should be worried, and then he had asked Jeffrey if he were thinking about taking his life, and if he were, he must talk to him about how he felt. Which was exactly the problem. One of the problems. The not talking. Dave had wept in that session, brokenhearted over Jeffrey, but Jeffrey had sat there and had even looked at his watch, not in a mean way, but still he had looked, not glanced, as his dad wept. Thomas had held his head in his hands which was a terrible thing to think about—an eleven-year-old boy in despair.

Jeffrey won't talk about his problems. He'll talk about other things that don't matter, like how his grandmom makes applesauce from the apples on the trees in her yard. Dr. Patel had said that was very nice, but that Jeffrey was talking about applesauce to avoid the real problem, "the elphant in dis rume, standing right here, swinging his trunk. Jeffrey, you must stop avoiding thees pachyderm." Then he had laughed, Darlene said that the doctor had laughed and laughed at his elephant joke. By pachyderm, the doctor meant the summons to court for contributing to the delinquency of minors. Chris and Tony were fifteen and seventeen. Twice Jeffrey had ignored the court dates, and now "your elphant has grown much beeger." Darlene could talk like Dr. Patel but without any meanness in her voice. She did not object to the joke about the elephant. It was too true, and now Jeffrey had two sets of problems with the law. He had left a case of beer and a bottle of whiskey on the counter in the kitchen, and then had gone to bed at a "decent hour" he told the doctor although he told the lawyer—Nell had gone to that session—that he had passed out. One-armed Chris and Tony had helped themselves, got drunk and then had driven home, that is, into a street sign as they tried to drive home. Jeffrey felt that he had been unjustly accused, that the teens had helped themselves to the booze while he was asleep/passed out. He did not ask Chris and Tony to drink, they just did. He did not even hear them come in the house or leave. All he knew was what he had heard later, that they did not make it home although the car was drivable after they hit the sign. Tony's mother reported him missing and when Tony was found, still drunk the next morning, she decided to have Jeffrey charged with contributing to Tony's delinquency. Chris' parents were not involved, and Nell wonders if this is why Jeffrey would like Chris if he had two arms. After this session, the suicide/elephant one, Jeffrey had announced that he would never go back to Dr. Patel. Thomas had said he would not either.

Darlene and Franklin are paying all the bills for the lawyer and the doctors. Also for the old car Jeffrey needs for his jobs. So far, the bills have mounted up to five thousand, give or take a few hundred. Jeffrey may get off if Tony's mom and lawyer don't show up for court next week, or Jeffrey could get a year in jail and/or a twenty-five-hundred-dollar fine, which Darlene will pay, if he is convicted. Darlene knows all the stories about what happens to young men, pretty young men like Jeffrey, in prison.

At seventy-five, Darlene is a devout Christian, a Republican, a retired third-grade teacher. She's never even tasted whiskey or been in a bar, but she watches

TV—*Dateline* and *Forty-Eight Hours*—and knows about prison rape. Nell is fifteen years younger and not sure about anything now that Richard has come home at least for two weeks this time, having failed at his suicide attempts, and so far refusing to go to a doctor, so it makes her feel good to be with Darlene, her longtime friend, who is certain that all of what is happening to Jeffrey and to them makes sense even though it may not seem to. All we have to do is hand our problems over to the Lord, she says.

Dr. Thia is not a tough love shrink. Darlene asked him that in his phone call about the family visit. He does not say as Dr. Patel had, "If Jeffrey were my son, I would have let him go to jail to concentrate on his problems until the court date. You better believe it. Two months or nine months. I would not have posted bail." Dr. Patel had asked Jeffrey how he thought he would feel about his mom and his grandmom and his little brother coming to see him in jail.

Jeffrey had shifted in his chair, Darlene told Nell, and said that he was sure that he would resent it because he felt that he had done nothing wrong. He seemed to miss the point about the shame they'd feel.

That afternoon, Dr. Thia stares at Jeffrey. "We must find out if you, Jeffrey, are a lazy young man, or if you, in fact, can't help yourself. Your Auntie here," he gestures toward Nell, "seems to feel that there is a condition in you that will not allow you to speak about what is wrong. But I know of no such condition, no such mental illness. One that ties up the tongue, as you might say." He had laughed at his little piece of psychiatric wisdom.

Nell has not said anything about how she feels about Jeffrey's being able to talk, but Dr. Thia has gotten pretty close to the truth somehow. He smiles gently, forgiving Jeffrey's ignorance and Nell's surprise that he can read her thoughts, forgiving her for being Jeffrey's Auntie who is ineffectual but sweet.

"The only way that medical science has, to date, for finding out whether or not a person is ill or immature or lazy or whatever, is to let him go out in the world and see how he does. Yes, you must have food. You must have a car. Not money for food. Just food. Not money for a car or gas, just the car and gas." He goes on, a sing-song description of the ideal life for Jeffrey, ending with little questions. This sounds like tough love to Nell. She can see Darlene shifting in her chair and Thomas is sprawled in his as if he has been tortured and flung there to die.

"Jeffrey, you have your new job at Target, no? So, you must give up the video games, right? You will set the alarm clock, yes? You will get out of bed and work eight hours a day, right? At least eight hours a day, good!" At twenty-three, the doctor smiles sweetly, a young man can work ten hours a day, easily, as he himself had done.

Nell would like to see what Dr. Thia would do to help Richard with his problems. The relief she feels with Darlene and Jeffrey's problems is like a shot of what, cocaine? Even if they reject the help, it's still help. Nell feels as if she is now thinking like Jeffrey: Even if Chris had two arms, she'd like him.

So today Nell has driven with Jeffrey, Paula, Darlene and Thomas to meet Dr. Thia. She understands that her role

51

is to be the aide, a silent partner, the secret sharer, the Auntie, on this first family visit to his new doctor, the one they hope is a soft-love doctor, the replacement she's found for Dr. Patel, the one Jeffrey'd been going to for two years, the one who'd almost persuaded Paula and Dave, backed up by Dave's parents, Darlene and Franklin, to kick Jeffrey out. Jeffrey had said that Dr. Patel had been a waste of their time and money and convinced them.

So maybe Nell is doing someone some good. Not her husband Richard from the way things have been going—but he is here for two weeks—and not for Jeffrey or his grandmother, her good friend Darlene. But maybe Nell and Thomas are getting some help, peripheral, from the doctor. Jeffrey's situation does take Nell's mind away from her own life with Richard, one that is getting worse as it gets clearer, as if it were being wrapped tighter and tighter in clear plastic sheets. Richard is drifting away, rather driving away in the night, coming back two days later, not knowing, he says sometimes, that he's been away. He smiles gently and goes to bed after being out all night. They now owe ten thousand on credit cards; the re-fi had taken care of sixty. But he has come home for two weeks. This fact about the ten thousand, Nell has just learned, just figured out from the calls from the credit card companies. She did not know about the new credit cards until one of the collection agents had agreed to talk to her against the company's policy. And the apartment feels like an oven as Richard trembles, chilled to the bone.

Nell may be called on to drive them home if Jeffrey looks as if he's "messed up his meds," the expression Darlene uses to explain a variety of problems Jeffrey has. If Jeffrey says he needs to sleep, Nell is to take the wheel immediately.

It's a long drive and the traffic can be bad. Jeffrey calls the shots because he's the one who's had what the Dr. Patel had called "a break." All the normal people, his family and Nell, do what Jeffrey says just as Nell does what Richard says, only Richard doesn't even have to say anything for Nell to keep their little boat floating. She makes the calls, borrows against insurance policies, cuts the heat off and lets the vent system run so Richard thinks the heat is on—anything she can think of to help. And, of course, it's not helping, but she is not in denial. She knows she's in trouble and that they are waiting for the axe to fall, an axe of some kind at some time, but maybe not for two weeks.

Darlene calls everyone else except her little group who have been to Dr. Patel and now Dr. Thia, the "untreated." Nell knows from her own life that it's the crazier person who has all the power though Richard acts as if he is the sanest person around, the one being brave. Like it's Nell who needs help, and like he's a victim of her world view which can be reduced to childish definitions: night is night and day is day, hot is hot, cold is cold. Too obvious, he says. One is for sleeping, one is for living. It's too simple, and it's wrong. He adds that it's killing him, these simple divisions of the world that Nell insists on imposing on him.

Dr. Patel had tried to put a stop to their bowing down to Jeffrey. He had told Darlene, who told Nell, not to give Jeffrey any more money for MacDonald's, for anything. Nell had started slipping five dollar bills in his shirt pocket to show that she was on his side until Darlene had said the doctor suspected their support strategies and told them no more treats, especially money, unless it was for cutting Darlene's grass. Darlene had smiled when she reported this to Nell. She cut her own grass. Jeffrey has said he would cut her grass, but so far, no, he has not cut a blade. Jeffrey had never even opened the door for Nell at Darlene's when she came over. Once he had asked her if she wanted a cup of coffee and when she said yes, he had indicated the automatic pot with some cold breakfast coffee.

When Nell had gotten to Darlene's house for this trip to Dr. Thia's, she and Jeffrey had stood in the driveway, awkward and trapped in the circumstances.

"Did you think we were going to an amusement park?" Jeffrey had asked Nell. He had held his cigarette up close to his eyes as if he were not exactly sure what it was that he was holding, this thing that was burning and dropping ashes on his shoes, studying the way fire and tobacco and paper work together to move toward the filter. His fingers and half-shut eyes said this might be his last smoke before he was prepared for the long walk down the corridor to the lethal injection room. His question was directed upward into the July blankness over Nell's head. Not to her. Not even at her.

Nell had looked down. His shoes were too big by at least two sizes and they were the wrong kind of shoes, old wingtips, him with shoulder-length hair as lustrous as an old-movie Indian's.

Nell and Darlene are "excellent hopers" Jeffrey has told them. He calls his grandmother Darli, and doesn't call Nell anything. She had been afraid that he might call her Nelly, but so far for two years, nothing. Nell had studied his vintage wingtips—he had on two pairs of socks. She moved up to the cuffs of his linen trousers, up the uneven creases to the leather belt. She hated herself for falling in with the general criticism of Jeffrey, all the things she had heard about him, and now here she was seeing all the things that are wrong with him. She knew some of his problems at first hand from her efforts to launch him in the local community college, the unspoken hope that being enrolled (even if not attending) would help keep him from going to jail. It didn't, and he was in weekend jail now, but Target has hired him anyway.

"All he needs is a yacht. He's been raised like a damned Kennedy," Franklin had said to Nell in one of their early talks about Jeffrey. He had liked all the tough-love advice from Dr. Patel and has no faith in this new man, another Indian who was impossible to understand.

"A damned Kennedy" is his summary of Jeffrey's problems. Franklin is sick to death of talking and hearing about Jeffrey and that's how Nell fits into the puzzle. She takes some of the heat off Franklin because Darlene talks to Nell about Jeffrey's condition/situation. Franklin can't take any more talking, and Dave can't either, father and son agree on this one thing. Still, Dave has not kicked Jeffrey out of the house. He tried to, or says he did, Franklin says.

Paula and Dave could not bring themselves to do what Dr. Patel had prescribed. They had got Jeffrey as far as the sidewalk in front of their house where he had sat on his suitcase until midnight and then gone around to his bedroom window and come back in. The next morning Darlene called Nell crying and asking her for help. Could she find them a new doctor, a better one? This is when Nell found Dr. Thiagarajah in the yellow pages.

Dr. Thia seems pleased to the same degree with everything Jeffrey tells him in the long summary of his life, whether it is appearing in court, enrolling in the community college classes, serving his weekend sentence, or discussing any of the plans for his life, like going into the army or starting his own plumbing business.

Nell fights being negative but Jeffrey has a snowball's chance at either plumbing or the military. Darlene has told Jeffrey in front of Nell that in the army, he would have to get up early in the morning, ditto for a plumbing business, plus, she told him, plumbers have to study water systems and work as apprentices. He can't just "be" a plumber, and anyway, how would he buy the truck he describes as having a sign on its side in fancy Gothic lettering—Jeffrey's Pipes.

If Dr. Thia works out for Jeffrey, Darlene says, she will never worry about anything again, that's how desperate she is for help. No need to rush anything else like keeping a job or going to school. Dave, she says, is on hold and doesn't expect anything at this point. He is this close to writing Jeffrey off. He thinks Jeffrey will be the old crazy guy around town, the one everyone knows, the first suspect in any child molestation cases, the man who never left home. Dave thinks that he and Paula will have to support Jeffrey all his life until they die. Then, he'll be a ward of the state.

Darlene has given Nell the account of Jeffrey's breakdown and his two-week stay in the psychiatric unit. The drive Darlene made to the hospital in western North Carolina with Jeffrey and Paula. Dave had been too upset to go with them. Franklin too. In fact, Darlene said, she couldn't really tell who should have been going to the hospital that day, Jeffrey or Dave, but Dave had helped get Jeffrey in the car, both of them sobbing. After he was admitted, Jeffrey had refused to leave the room he was put in for a week. The relief that the Zoloft gave him, he could not deny, and after a week, he had come out of his room and taken part in the therapies and activities. Still, he felt a great reluctance to take the medicine. Dr. Patel had made sense to Darlene she said until it came time for Paula and Dave to open their door and push Jeffrey out with no money, no food, nothing. They had tried, but Jeffrey had no skills except in video games. Jeffrey does not know how to survive Darlene says. If he does not do what he has promised <u>her</u>, his grandmother, his Darli, the one who has made him pancakes in the middle of the afternoon, hot cocoa and cheese toast, after not cutting her grass and not pruning the shrubs, how can he keep a job or get one. The Target job is a miracle. But when Nell and Darlene had found the Target ad and written the email application for Jeffrey, a phone call had come almost immediately, and in three days, Jeffrey was working the graveyard shift. Two weeks! He has worked two whole weeks! The world can change!

Dr. Thia says when Jeffrey finishes his summary of his life, that he wants them to never use one word again in their lives. He does not seem to have taken in Jeffrey's story, but he must have, of course. It's the word "but." It's a curse word, he says. "If" and "then" are also dangerous words. For instance, "if Jeffrey <u>could</u> not do what he had promised her, his grandmother, then how could he keep a job?" That is the wrong way to understand the problem. The first part does not go with the second part. They have nothing to do with each other. "But" is the worst word. They must use "and" when they talk about Jeffrey. Nell tries it out: "Jeffrey went to his grandmother's, had pancakes <u>and</u> did not cut the grass." It does sound better than "<u>but</u> did not cut the grass." Jeffrey seems to like the new doctor.

In her head, Nell tries this rule of "no buts, ifs or thens" out on her life with Richard: He drove all night somewhere <u>and</u> did not tell her where he had gone, <u>and</u> went to work the next day. He has spent seventy thousand dollars <u>and</u> did not mention it to her, <u>and</u> he turns the heat on in July. It does help <u>and</u> keeps life livable.

It is wrong simply to say that Jeffrey breaks promises and has dropped out of school. Or failed the papers Nell helped him write for his classes, though Nell wonders if he really turned them in or if the teacher suspected too much help on them and failed him as the better alternative to reporting him for an honor court violation. It was hard to write about <u>Lord Jim</u> if a person hated words as much as Jeffrey did. Nell had tried to catch Jeffrey's flat, silent style in the essay when she helped him with/wrote his essay out on Darlene's porch.

She knows that if she had not insisted on his writing the essay that Jeffrey would not have written it, and would have failed out sooner. She would have given that paper she wrote a C- in her own freshman comp class, but/and she knows that she gives high grades. Jeffrey's essays were failures by the old standards, old, meaning five years ago, but/and by the new standards they were at best C-'s.

Since Nell and Richard had moved into Darlene's country/suburban neighborhood on the outskirts of Raleigh—another new job for Richard, the third in five years—she has been in on the whole Jeffrey thing—the new medicines, the new plans, everything. And, now this new doctor for Jeffrey.

Nell had laughed her back-pedaling laugh at Jeffrey's amusement park question and retreated from the troubled young man lounging against the old Escort in the sun. He was claiming the privilege of ironic questioning of motive, of commenting on Nell's shabby charity. A very Conradian move. He reminds Nell of Richard, and that is not good. Jeffrey is certainly seeing right through Nell and had skewered her hope this afternoon for distraction from her anxieties about Richard. Jeffrey probably had gotten the whole story of Richard's problems down pat from a few bored glances at Richard when Nell introduced him. Like Franklin, Richard can't stand to hear any more about Jeffrey, and Richard is not Jeffrey's grandfather. And, he is sorry for Darlene, sorry for Franklin, for Paula, for Dave, for Thomas, and he is sick to death, he has said, of Jeffrey.

After the amusement park question, Nell had lowered her arms held up for the hug she was going to give Jeffrey, moving in backward steps alongside the vibrating car around the hot engine to the driver's side, patting the car as she moved, as if it needed comfort because it certainly was not taking them to any amusement park. Nell was hoping that this would be the low point, the worst thing that would happen during the afternoon. She did not let herself hope that Jeffrey would throw a crazy fit right then and refuse to let her go. Or say he was not going himself. Where was all that sobbing she had heard Darlene talk about? At that point, the amusement park point, Nell had felt that she'd been distracted enough from Richard's problems and now she would like to go back home to the apartment. She wouldn't have minded Jeffrey's calling her a few names, though that was not Jeffrey's style which she knew very well. Bemused questioning was his M. O.

She had heard the story of how when he was twelve, he refused to move when his family moved. He stayed in the old farm house and lived there three months until the new people told him they were calling social services about an abandoned child or the sheriff if he weren't out by the next day. So, if he did not want Nell, the old-lady school teacher friend of his Darli, the interfering friend/tenant of his grandmother, to go with him to his psychiatrist, this new doctor she was forcing him to go to, he did not have to let her go or go himself. Why couldn't he just go sit on his Darli's porch and refuse to get in the car until this Nell person left? Nell hoped that she was channeling his thoughts and she urged him telepathically to do what he wanted to do. Not go. Let her off the hook.

Nell pinned her Plan B hopes on Paula whose window she had now reached in her patting move around the car, the long-suffering Paula, who is sitting in the driver's seat but moved when Jeffrey gave her a silent signal: He would drive the first lap. Maybe Paula would say that there was no need for Nell to go with them, that actually they would be crowded in the little Escort if she did go, that Nell might have something she had to do instead of giving them her whole afternoon. As if Paula would want to miss out on an excursion to an amusement park with this assortment of five people. Nell goes down the list as she tries praying for Plan B. The deeply Christian grandmother, Darlene, who was confident that she would not be Left Behind when the world ended and was anxious about the spiritual state of her family;

Jeffrey, the Kennedy; his mother, Paula, Thomas, faithful follower of Jeffrey; and then, the fifth wheel Nell, fifty-nine-year-old freshman comp teacher and fifth year college senior tutor friend and tenant of Darli, the Nell who was sticking her nose in their family's business to avoid her own business of her nutcase husband.

What amusement park in the world could even Darlene's God find for this group? Paula at forty-five collects memorabilia of movie stars. A life-size James Dean figure stands in her and Dave's bedroom, a fact that might account for some of Jeffrey's trouble, or the tiny dogs who bite at Nell when she walks in the dark house, who bark like crazy, or the silence that governs the family and emanates from deep inside the Paula-Dave marriage. Paula is embittered <u>and</u> is also a reluctant survivor of lymphoma. The family acts as if they are deaf people who refuse to use sign language. They need to start over but/and how can they? Nell knows that she does not have any room to talk, her with her own life.

Jeffrey may be schizophrenic—the doctor at the hospital had said that he was, another one said that he was borderline. Dr. Patel was not sure. Dr. Thia has not had his turn.

Jeffrey has something of a point in his question about the amusement park, and she freely admits that they do seem to be setting off for an afternoon of fun. All they need is a wicker hamper of ham and cheese sandwiches on rye and pumpernickel, a jug of sweetened tea and some chips. Or they might buy hotdogs when they got to the park. For such an outing, an excursion, they would need some conversation.

Yes, they'd need to buy some stuff for such an excursion.

Had Jeffrey's question been a comment on Nell's outfit? Her jeans and tee shirt ironed thirty minutes ago or her lime green tennis shoes and straw tote bag? Was he protesting the fact that she had set this whole waste of time in motion, and then had the nerve, the juice to be going with him and his family? Horning in again. He might think that Nell has done enough harm. He had not been the one who asked her to go today though he had asked her to go before—"You can go if you want to"—on other trips to admissions offices, financial aid offices, interviews, an attorney's office and once to Dr. Patel's. She had always gone, for Darlene's sake and more and more lately, for her own sake.

Thomas has been twisting around and around on shoes whose heels and soles light up, first on one foot, in one direction, then on the other foot, reversing on a dime, blinking red and green, getting drunk. He twirls on Darlene's asphalt drive in slow motion, going crazy with these adults he's trapped with. "Sweet chance," Nell thinks she hears him gasp to Jeffrey's question to her about the amusement park. He goes into a bitter spin that tips him over onto the hot, soft asphalt of the driveway. He and Jeffrey talk more than anyone else in their family, but it's all in video game code. Nell can't understand a word they say.

When Nell pats the Escort's fender up to Paula in this nervous gesture she is developing—patting car fenders—Paula implied by leaning on the door to open it, and beginning to swing her knees outward that she wants to get out. In fact, she seems to be saying that she won't go herself if only Nell would offer to drive with Jeffrey to the doctor and drive him home if he needs her to, if his meds mess him up. Would Nell do that for them? It is a silent, powerful question. Paula unbuckles and makes a more direct move to open the door. Then, if Nell would go in her place, there would be only four people going, if Paula does not have to go, and four is the right number for the Escort on the thirty-seven mile trip over to the Counseling Center. All in silent language. Paula does get out, responding to Jeffrey's saying he would drive.

Nell shakes her head no to both Jeffrey and Paula. She is supposed to be going in Dave's place, isn't she? She is beginning to get the hang of the way they do not talk because they don't need to. The questions they ask are so ridiculous. No answers are needed. Would a relative stranger take her son to the shrink, the son who has just asked a sarcastic question to the kind person named Nell?

No, Nell telepaths to Jeffrey and Thomas, she does not think she is going to Kings Park today to go on the monster rides, and no, to Paula, she won't go in her place. Yes, she beams to Darlene, she would go in Dave's place.

Nell thinks of her and Richard's daughters who are working in St. Louis and Chicago, keeping their own kind of silence which translates into "I'm fine, Mom. How's Dad this week? No, I'll call if I need anything." Darlene often implies that Nell is lonely for her children and thinking about Jeffrey is, in its way, a lift for Nell's spirits. She's right.

On the ride to Dr. Thia's, Jeffrey drives and smokes. Darlene and Nell sit in the back. It is ninety-three degrees on the bank clock as they turn toward the by-pass. Nell had turned the heat off when she left home. Darlene tells Jeffrey that the wind is ruining her hair which she had just curled and that the smoke is bad for her throat. He lets his window up two inches without looking back at her in the rearview mirror.

Paula announces that she never uses the air conditioning because it takes too much gas which has just gone up again. Darlene says that she will pay for the gas if Paula will turn on the air conditioning. Paula says she is not sure it still works.

This is more talk than Nell has ever heard from Paula. Thomas kicks his shoes so they light up and he reaches for the AC dial. There is a rush of hot, hot air, but then it cools down and they ride in a deeper silence.

Dr. Thia's office is full and they have to break up to find seats across the room and into an alcove. There are emergency cases who get called in before them. A man is rocking forward almost out of his seat while his son holds him so he won't topple, his arm draped around his father's shoulder, as if they are friends, drunk and glad to have found a park bench. Their three-thirty appointment drifts by and it is four forty-five when they file into Dr. Thia's office.

Good Afternoon, Mrs. Herndon

It was late in the afternoon, the sun was level with our car window, not blinding us, but giving the person looking down in at us a brilliant black outline. Mrs. Walton blazed in the physics of the sunshine and in the glory of herself. She was at her mailbox getting her letters and her Boston newspaper. The mailbox was in the middle of the big dangerous curve and her house, designed for one of Jefferson's poor cousins, set uphill from it, staring grandly at the creek a mile away on the low grounds. My great uncle had lived there once, briefly, and had had all the boxwoods dug up so he could "see the river," better.

We were veering toward Mrs. Walton, swooping in. She was looking through her letters, not worried about being killed. Daddy gave the steering wheel a masterful touch and just brushed Mrs. Walton's tennis skirt, the only one in the county, as he came to a gentle stop.

There were many things wrong with the picture I was trapped in at fourteen in central Virginia. It had been years since we had moved to the country, and I should have been used to it. Mama loved to tell me "Iron bars do not a prison make." I would answer her "What do they make?" which made her smile sadly, but proud of what she sometimes called my "seeing into the life of things" or at other times, my "spunkiness."

Daddy was drunk in his middle-of-the-week way, still driving, of course, in spite of his neck brace from his latest and worst wreck six months ago. He hadn't gone back to work yet, so was free to drive me to Alice's house for Friday night, Saturday, Saturday night and all day Sunday if I could swing it, staying until I was taken or brought home, having stayed until even I could not stay any longer. "Don't you need a change of clothes? Should we call your mother?" Alice's mother had blue blood. So did mama, but of a lighter blue. She was not a direct descendant of Pocahontas and John Rolfe.

At Alice's there was always ice cream and cold fried chicken, a record player and perfect freedom. Daddy would be sober enough to come get me starting on Saturday, but too mad at the world to do it. Drinking, he was putty in my hands. As he drank, my chances improved for a social life, and mama's went downhill. And the weekend stretched in front of me full of the great pleasures of being with Alice in her beautiful old home filled with mirrors and walnut "pieces" from her ancestors.

Our muddy Vauxhall had a bent frame from the accident that had broken daddy's neck—not that we knew it was broken for three days when I, without a driver's license, had driven him to the hospital in Richmond for an x-ray, mama's saying all the time as she held daddy's head straight from the backseat with a pillow folded over it and his head in an arm lock, his chin set into her elbow, that I was doing a good job, and that Edward, a better driver, was too young at twelve for the fifty-mile trip. Daddy had said "Take it easy, dammit." He never said it hurt.

So I had driven us to the hospital, veering to the side of the road, correcting with little jerks of the steering wheel.

"Don't jerk the wheel so damn hard," is what daddy said sober as a judge that day on the way to the x-ray machine. Drunk, he would have smiled encouragingly.

His driver's side window was rolled down half the way, another result of the accident. We coasted to a stop, kissing the hem so to speak of Mrs. Walton's pale orange skirt. She found herself distracted from her friends' letters and the Boston headlines by our sudden appearance and without meaning to be that friendly to us, her neighbors from two miles up the road in a house Jefferson's much poorer cousins made do in, she had bent down and stared in through the window at us.

Daddy still wore his fedora, left over from his days in a Washington government office and his wire-rimmed glasses repaired many times. Neither the hat nor the glasses went with his carpenter's coveralls, and now he doffed his hat to Mrs. Walton, though there was hardly any head room to doff in. "Good afternoon, Mrs. Herndon," he said, smoothly, as if he were back in his office speaking to his secretary. Mrs. Herndon was the opposite of Mrs. Walton, opposite in type and in every detail. As far from a person who wore a tennis skirt and had friends in New England as it's possible to be. She could put up a hundred quarts of green beans after she had picked them that morning, after she had grown them all summer and hoed the weeds. That night she would make a cake to take to church and then as an afterthought, some biscuits to go with the ham she'd slice off the one she kept in the refrigerator. She weighed two hundred pounds, used curse words and told dirty jokes. She and Mr. Herndon and their three frightening children were tenants on Mrs. Walton's farm, and her face in God's eyes and daddy's that day did have a certain broad similarity, but no sober person on earth could have ever confused the two. Ten years later, I would learn that Mrs. Walton had dessert plates with French puns written around the hand-painted scenes. As always, I tried to disappear. To melt into the door, emerge as a smear of blood and hair on the other side and lie quietly in the weeds by the side of the road waiting for my remains to be identified years from the terrible now of my life. But the Vauxhall's door was made of reinforced steel, one of its admirable features daddy liked to point out, and recently said it had saved his life if not his neck.

I had seen my new home for the first time when I was almost five years old. It made me know early in life that I was the child of crazy people though I hoped I was adopted.

Crazies. Both of them. My parents. Lovable but dangerous. Much later, I would try to understand daddy's dependence on vodka and mama's denial of their vodka-soaked life, and her insistence that we were living another kind of life. For mama, iron bars were invisible and did not make a prison, no indeed.

That day the four of us, my doomed family, had walked almost a mile from the state road. The track had the faint traces of a drive, grown over ruts—if it was ox carts you had to drive in— even with all the paradise trees. When we came to a rise that seemed to signal an approach to a dwelling of ogres, I couldn't see any sign of a house in the mountain of green.

"Where is it? Our house?" I asked. "There," mama said and pointed to a thicker, taller greener clump of trees. "Right there, Nell, in front of you."

That was in the late summer of 1948 when we moved to the country, away from a rock house with apple and sycamore trees in its long back yard near Washington to an old farmhouse on two hundred and sixty-seven acres in central Virginia on the James River. My family was one whose problems were planted deep in their pasts, but the move brought them to the surface and made them worse. For my younger brother Edward, it worked out better, not that it was easy for him. This was in the dark ages before there was a general understanding of denial, before anyone knew about compensatory fantasies, long before I grew up to marry a liar, one I loved with all I had in me, which meant I came to understand some of my parents' lies and a few of my own.

I was in this way—an old hand at misrepresentations of all kinds—perfect for Richard.

Edward was my deadly enemy when we were children, but my rescuer when we were older and Richard went crazy. Our parents loved each other but were almost completely wrong for each other. "Almost" because they also had what they called their "elective affinities" that were wonderful, and it was these that I came to feel were the most important of all things on earth. To feel mama's admiration for daddy when he quoted the opening of Walter Scott's "Marmion," ignoring the fact that he was drunk, made me, but not Edward, admire all things poetic or if those things were in scarce supply, all things Scottish, and by tenuous association, made me marry Richard. Admiring such a talent was more important than any other fact like heat in the house when the pipes froze. I learned this way of seeing people and the world from mama.

Later the wrongness of these views, that is, their clanging-clashing, became clearer when daddy voted for Nixon and mama wrote in her choice for president, Dr. Benjamin Spock. She explained to me that he had changed the way children were seen and treated, and that we should feel very fortunate that she had had the opportunity to study early childhood with Dr. Spock. For one thing, we didn't have to say "sir" and "mam" to our aunts and uncles the way our cousins did, a terrible holdover, she said, from slavery. The cousins thought we didn't know any better, and their parents blamed mama for ruining her children. What good would her master's degree in nursing do her when her children grew up to be criminals? Mama had been in Cleveland in the late 1930's, that time when she might have decided not to marry daddy.

As a boy, he had visited a farm once, but mama had grown up on the one seven miles up the river from the old farm house we were living in. He knew nothing about country life, she knew everything. How to make sauerkraut, lye soap, damson preserves, apple butter, dried apples. The move was not a good beginning. I vaguely felt it, but forgot it in the compensations of the shallow river half a mile away from the house, sandy on the bottom with a muddy bank with its roots sticking out for handles to hold to as I climbed down into the clear brown current.

Undaunted by reality, we moved to the country.

We lied to ourselves about what we were heading into. Alcoholism, for one thing. Daddy was lying to himself about what a friend he had found in vodka, mama about the joys that country life would give us, though there were demi-joys—the river and the old horses on our cousins' farm, the tractors and trucks, the hay barns. Mama treated me and Edward as if we were gifts from heaven—here she had to lie blatantly. About me anyway. From daddy I learned a lesson that was more complicated: there are ways to soften reality and let others take the hit. No need for big lies. Little ones are more convincing.

Our new home had been built in 1820, its central group of rooms, at least, had been. It was situated wrong: not staring down over the fields to the river and not up through the overgrown fields to the state dirt road. Oddly angled away from both river and road, or as I later thought of it, away from any possibility of escaping, it was as if the house had been dropped from a crane up in the sky by a drunk person.

Later, I would find out that the house had been moved closer to the road from its original site on the river bluff. The movers, the freed children of slaves, must have walked off the job to look for better work because they left the house where they stopped in 1866, the news of emancipation taking over a year to come the sixty-seven miles from Appomattox—not trying to gee and haw the mules harnessed to the contraption of logs the house had been set on in order to roll it down from the bluff closer to the new-at-the-time state road. The slaves who built the pyramids couldn't have been any smarter than the black men who moved our ten room house half a mile away from the river. It was the house they themselves had built or their grandparents had with hand sawn weatherboarding and put together with homemade nails and sometimes with pegs.

In the eighth grade, I read "The Fall of the House of Usher" and understood the poor narrator's first glimpse of the friend's home he was visiting, the sinking feeling as he looked at the old pile across the tarn. The dead sister and dying brother waiting to ruin his life and scare the bejesus out of him. It became my favorite story and I used it to teach freshman composition, somehow, later. One student, a black man, even won an essay prize for his essay on the story, something about how we never know what will happen on a visit to friends.

When we got closer that day when we first saw the house, the trees seemed to be growing out of it, the clump mama had pointed to as the house. By that first winter, daddy had cut down the paradise and locust trees in the long driveway, but we had to leave the car up at the mailbox because the mud was so deep we couldn't drive the car through it. If we tried to get the car up to the house after a heavy rain, we got stuck. Always, this happened until Edward started driving at seven. He had a way of fording the mud, riding the ridges between the ruts, as if the car were a motorboat, and he wasn't afraid of hurting the engine the way mama and daddy were.

The school bus would cut its engine and wait for us to run the quarter mile to get on. By the time I was in the third grade and Edward in the first, mama was running with us. She was teaching the first grade, her training in nursing (with Dr. Spock) put on the shelf and never mentioned though she used it to treat the injuries school children have and to try to help the more terrible things they suffered at home, the ones she could see in the bruises under their clothes. One little girl with such bad headaches she twirled herself around and around. Mama sent her to Richmond to a doctor who found that she had a brain tumor which killed her in a few weeks. Several had polio. Mama helped set up medical and dental clinics every fall. The sexual abuses she had to let pass as there was no one to report them to.

I was still not able to read when I was eight, maybe because I had been terrified of the thirty-seven children in the first grade who had all grown up in the country. But I knew how to pretend to read and could memorize anything. Thank God for social promotion and for the skills in mendacity I was learning at mama's knee so that it seemed that I was reading and somehow along with several others, I was passed into the second and then the third grade where I finally did learn to see the connection between the black lines and circles and the words I had heard and used for years. In the first grade, I learned only to steal candy when it was sold after lunch on a table in our classroom for the whole school—about two hundred and twenty children. Handing out the stolen Almond Joys or rolls of Necco Wafers or some Mary Janes worked miracles and won me a few friends for that day. One day, mama took me to the teacher who sold the candy and said that she wanted to give the teacher something. It was an envelope with money to pay for my stolen candy. I handed it over pretending it was a letter, and then I ran out of the room hoping I would trip and break my neck and be carried away to a hospital where I would be mixed up, like babies sometimes were, and sent to another family far away. Or would be diagnosed with a brain tumor and could die soon.

Edward adjusted to our new life in the country, and by November of his first grade could read, as one relative put it, "like a top." By seven, he was driving the car like a top as well as doing other things like a top like hunting rabbits, squirrels and turkeys. His method of avoiding getting stuck in our driveway was, he explained, simple: "Speed makes power." He would gun the car up to about forty and then it would almost fly through the mud making a roaring noise which confirmed his understanding of the problem.

His success in the first grade and with the car in the mud gave him a life-long regard for the truth: tell it quickly and it gives you the power to get to your destination. Or, in situations where I would immediately lie, he would simply refuse to speak. Later, he was the one who said to daddy, shooting him between the eyes, that he was going for treatment whether he agreed to it or not. Then, he put daddy in the car and took him to the center where he dried out. It worked several times. But along with mama, I would deny that there were problems with the drinking, that there had been wrecks and debts, even a child run over and taken to the hospital, even daddy's own neck broken in a one-car accident and six weeks in traction, a barn burned down by a slowly tossed cigarette by his weaving and stumbling away from the hay-filled loft. During those years, I saw myself as an equestrienne (without horse) or a ballerina (without bar or slipper).

Two large rooms of the house were falling away from that center core of eight rooms. It was that center core that had balanced on the logs rolling down from the bluff to where it now sat. The front porch barely attached across the front, had a sleeping porch upstairs. The place had never been farmed with tractors, just mules and slaves, and later, with mules and hired men. Only our cousins owned tractors.

The great-great granddaughter of one of those slaves, the old man we called Uncle Bonaparte, was Peaches Johnson who was the same age as me. Her grandfather had been born a slave on the place and would laugh and shake his head when we asked him what it had been like during slavery. This question came to me when I was in the fourth grade and had a unit on Virginia history. Slavery was mentioned as an event in 1619, one or two sentences. Uncle Bonaparte died when I was in the seventh grade, "somewhere over a hundred." He used to say he couldn't tell no white people anything about "none of that time, about none of the stories he had listened to as a little thing from his old peoples. They was too sad." White people, he told me, couldn't stand to hear sad stories. They would be too cut up by them.

He was a boy when his family was freed but they stayed on working on the place. Nothing changed for them very much. Peaches and her family lived near Uncle Bonaparte's cabin in a frame house a mile from us. As soon as they could, in the late 1950's, they had moved to Philadelphia where Peaches was killed when she was a teenager. We heard about it five years after it happened and thought it must have been the gang violence we were reading about in the newspaper. One of Peaches' cousins from Philly, he called it, visited her family in the summers, Charles Durand. He used to ride their old white horse around, sticking a rusty nail in his rump to make him buck so he'd look like a cowboy. I could imagine gangs made up of Charles Durands. Peaches might not have had a better life in Virginia, but she would not have been murdered, mama said. Peaches was pretty and let me help her take care of her baby brothers Tyrone and Arthur, the ones

75

mama had delivered. Mama took Uncle Bonaparte's wife, the fierce Aunt Lucy, to the doctor for her gout.

Our new home had a twin house two miles up the river. It looked down on the river the right way, not dropped like ours, slipped off the rolling logs, and was called James View. There had been seventeen rooms before the slaves got the house on the logs to roll it closer to the state road, and it took daddy a couple of years to tear the two loosest rooms off. It wasn't hard because some of them were not attached securely to the main part of the house. We had to walk downhill a few steps to get into some of those rooms.

That first year we raised chickens in one of the front rooms. I knew that people did not live with chickens. We were the next occupants after 1918. Once I heard a hissing and it was a snapping turtle as big as a dinner plate with a long triangular tail in the front hall. Prehistoric.

I knew that mama and daddy had lost their minds, but I was trapped with them. They had left their nice rock house in the suburbs because daddy had lost his job with the government when all the veterans came home after 1945.

Maybe I had gone into what is now called childhood depression. I gave up any hope of having a family like the one I wanted and threw in the towel. I would adjust to this new life in the country if it killed me. On the good side of my new life, there was that table of candy just sitting there waiting to be stolen to bribe the first graders, all of whom had learned to read faster than I had. But there were no ice cream parties where people danced and then jumped in the river—these were the stories mama had told me to persuade me that our move to the country was a good thing and to shut down the screaming that started in my heart, worked its way up to my throat and then out into the air when I had looked down the hill toward the green hill where our new home was hidden.

Mama had lied to us about the move to the country. All those ice cream parties where people came and danced all night and then walked half a mile down to the river to go swimming to refresh themselves before they came back to a big country breakfast. Mama had put all my favorite words into that lie—ice cream, dancing and river. Her lies would get worse, but that's the one that made the move possible for me. Driving through the mud of our driveway did it for Edward. He loved his new life—mud, snapping turtles, snakes.

Mama had to lie to me to get me to leave the rock house in the city where daddy, sober as a judge, had once taken me to the circus and once to a movie. Mama's study with Dr. Spock had made her so much more lenient and understanding of children than was usual, and than her own childhood had been. She spanked us only once, each, me for dipping my braids in yellow paint and Edward for breaking five dozen eggs when he had been told by a cousin that there were gold coins in some of the eggs, but he'd have to break each one to find out which ones had the coins. So, when I started having a tantrum to prevent the move to the country, mama told me the lies about the ice cream and river and threw in the dancing.

I thought happiness was coming in new colors before we moved, before I saw our new home. For one thing, in the country, in a new life, I thought that I would somehow instantly be ten years older, beautiful, with a figure, know how to dance and talk to boys and how to swim. I was my own Cinderella movie starring myself.

"Your father is not drinking," was the governing lie that we came to live under. In the country, his drinking got worse. In the city drinking is different or people live with it better. Another lie was constructed especially for me: "You are not that kind of person." Maybe in the country, I had veered away from the kind of person mama had in mind for me.

The ice cream and dancing and river swims were minor league lies compared to the one about daddy's not drinking. Mama seemed to think that I could grow up into one of those voile-wearing girls, all worn out and frail from so much dancing and swimming and that I would marry one of the young men much later—a doctor who had trained somehow at Western Reserve, now called Case-Western Reserve University. She seemed to think that daddy was sober every weeknight as she helped him up the stairs.

Trained to lie myself, I would grow up to marry Richard, the liar of liars, actually two men, one who knew what he was doing and one who honestly did not know or thought that he did not know that he was planning at every move his suicide and had to conceal it from everyone, especially me. All this I learned much later from therapy.

Richard's death was ordained by his mother when he was three, but he held off until his mid-fifties. I was not the kind of person who had that kind of mother problem. No indeed, I was an equestrienne and ballerina who lived in a house with chickens and a snapping turtle and many snakes.

There were seven big rooms downstairs in our new/old house, not counting the two hardly attached ones that daddy tore off. The frantic and incessant peeping of the sixty baby chicks sounded like the two electrical appliances, a bathroom heater which we got that first winter and the clock on the kitchen Hot Point, gone haywire. At a distance and upstairs which had five big rooms and a short, wide hall, the sharp little sounds were absorbed in the heart pine flooring, so we could sleep. There was a rosewood piano in the room with the baby chickens and an old carved sofa which mama pointed out as good things, signs that we were in a good place. She said that Miss Mary Lou, the last owner who had lived there before the first world war—this would have been at the turn of the twentieth century which to me seemed the time when the Christians were tossed to the lions—had had the strawberry ice cream parties in this front room, and had played the piano for the dancing people and when they were tired of ice cream and dancing, "if you can imagine," mama would say, they would sit for a while on the green velvet sofa before they trekked down to the river holding up their dancing dresses. The men did not care what happened to their trousers because they were real men, who did not care about things like trousers getting drenched in the early morning dew, but they would care about the girls' hems getting wet and maybe they carried the girls through the heaviest dews and damps. Did they wear their bathing suits under the dresses the way I did on Sundays hoping, hoping that some older cousin would ask us to go swimming somewhere.

That was mama—thinking of the ice cream and strawberries and dancing as the baby chicks rushed to the corners of the room in a pale yellow cloud of fluff, leaving smelly streaks behind them on the layers of newspaper she had laid down for them. She certainly knew that ice cream took a great deal of work—she would milk a Holstein cow—her name was Sawbones—every morning and evening, separate the cream from the milk, make the custard, gather the eggs from her laying hens—it took sixteen eggs for the custard. She started a strawberry bed and knew how the plants depended on the right sun and rain and the weeding. She knew that making a voile dress or the dresses she would make me took at least a week of sewing an hour or two in the afternoons, her portable Singer plugged in the kitchen outlet. She knew how to work and could work circles around anyone—that was her reputation.

As all children of liars know, children will believe anything their parents tell them. In spite of hard evidence.

How could she tell the old feather cushions on the velvet sofa, now pale as straw, used to be green I asked mama. How did she know about the dancing parties? She knew, she said, because her third cousin told her, the one who used to be one of the girls who danced and helped Miss Mary Lou turn the crank on the ice cream freezer. "Not that old woman who is humped over and stinks," I had said, remembering the person we had gone to visit in the nursing home and tried to talk to. "That's the very one," her mama said. "She suffers from rheumatoid arthritis and osteoporosis, and she lost her farm to the bank. That's how we have come to have her house and farm."

Mama had married daddy, who was, in fact, an alcoholic, but only during the week. On weekends, he was stone cold sober and farmed the two hundred and sixty-seven acres they, in one of their mutual fits of denial, had bought for sixty-three hundred dollars from the old cousin. In 1948, that was a good deal, even for a house that was forty years old when the Civil War started. It had a tiny, little bit of electricity, about a quart of it, but had had those ice cream parties with the dancing and then the swimming in the river. Much better than electricity.

Mama grew up on a farm with cows, chickens, horses, and a garden that produced enough for grandma to sell her vegetables and send the money to Korean orphans. A farm had possibilities—that was one thing mama learned from her childhood of being out in the middle of nowhere. Daddy learned that fifty miles from Richmond, fifty from Charlottesville and a hundred and thirty from Washington meant that he was living far from alcohol supplies. He would have to go to the next county, twenty-three miles, to find the state liquor store. He did find bootleggers closer to us who were still in business in the 1950's.

Risk Management

At the rest stop just after Thomasville, Regina hears a voice behind her as she is stepping into her white Escort. "Ma'am, could you help me with my school project? You look like the kind of person who wouldn't mind answering a few questions. A nice person. It won't take long because I can see from your license plates that you are almost home. The Virginia line is thirty-eight miles from here. And it looks like you have been on a trip. From all the clothes bags in the back seat."

"I promise it won't take long. It's for my senior project and I have to have it done by tomorrow. My bad for waiting so long. It's called Risk Management and my assignment is to interview people at this rest stop of I-85 and find out how they manage risks or some damn thing like that."

Regina is a friendly person and not in a hurry—that's for sure—to get home. She likes driving and stopping at Wendy's or at the rest stops. After work, she goes out driving on the interstate, just to feel that she is going somewhere, like she is on a trip. She takes bottles of water and snacks as if the drive is long. And, she takes the little gun she got at the gun show for a hundred and thirty-three dollars. It makes her feel both dangerous and endangered, more interesting. Where is she driving? To where, St. Louis? New Orleans? Somewhere interesting, somewhere with criminals. Thirty-eight miles is one of her longer drives. She knows that she should not talk to this young man. Her body will be found, or not, months or years later. Or, maybe his will be. Dogs will find one of them or some hunter. Her pretty tattoo on the small of her back, the three butterflies, will be wasted, and just when they have lost their soreness and puffiness. He is a handsome boy, someone's his mom, someone loves him.

Then again, she's a runner, can sprint for half a mile, and run for five miles, jog along for ten. Nights she lifts weights in the school gym. She's a tough one her mom says. Her dad's been gone a while, maybe even five years now, but they don't miss him. Actually, it's a good thing.

No more surprises from her dad's credit cards or men driving up to the house leaving the motors running in their Mercedes or Navigators. People thought something with drugs was going on and probably they were right. Her dad was a man who expected and got women to love him which Regina and her mom certainly did, but they could not, repeat not, live with him.

Regina has her mom's prettiness, a fact confirmed by the famous NASCAR driver's grandson seeing her in the mall when his family was shopping for last minute stuff on their way to Florida and coming up to her and striking up a conversation by saying that she was the prettiest girl he had ever seen. "Don't know many then," she had laughed, knowing that she was making herself even prettier. Now they were texting each other, at least he was texting her and she'd send back a smile or something to keep him going. He said he wanted to ask her about evolution and creationism and if she were saved, but so far, he hadn't. She guessed he was a religious nut, but everyone was some kind of one, right? This kid asking her to help him with his stupid school project looked like a more interesting nutcase. She prided herself on not caring, deeply not caring about God. Not about global warming and the polar bears either. She had some interest in the Clintons' marriage and their sex lives which she'd read about. She knew that if this religious guy who had to be rich ever did come to see her at her house, not that she was there all that much, he would never get out of his car, and that would be a what? Maybe a Mustang, a safe car for a rich man's grandson.

But, Regina cannot resist being asked questions about herself. And the other side of that—telling people what she knows. She knows she talks too much and about things that number one are nobody's business and number two could be dangerous, and now she hears herself say what she shouldn't. "I shouldn't be talking to you for the simple reason that I already know four murderers. But, since you asked, I mean I could tell you wanted to, all those murderers killed people they knew, just like the experts say on TV. I don't know of any strangers killing people. You would be my first."

"Man, Pretty Lady," the boy with the notebook said slowly, "You sure know how to creep a guy out. That's the first time I have ever been called a killer to my face. Killer, meaning, you know, stab, stab, or shoot, shoot, or maybe choke, choke. Now, my girlfriend calls me a killer but in the good sense, if you know what I mean."

Regina knows what he means, not from having what she calls to herself real sex itself, just some "encounters" that were not all that great. She smiles. He asks her to tell him about the four murderers, forget the survey for his project. What she knows is more interesting than the idiot assignment. She can't resist. She remembers assignments like this one from high school which is why she quit for a few weeks, but pretended to still be going, and when it got almost too late to go back without repeating a year, she went. It's been two years since then. She tells him the murders in chronological order.

"When I was six, the preacher, not at the church I went to, went crazy and killed his wife and mother-in-law with an axe and was coming to get his little girl, who was my friend, and who was actually that very night, sleeping over at my house."

"Crazy killers don't count," the boy smiled his handsome smile. He had dark brown eyes and three earrings in each ear. His tee shirt had the sleeves cut out to show his tattoos. An eagle and a heart.

"Right. If you are going to be that way. Then when I was eight, a neighbor shot his wife, his aunt and a neighbor. Do those count?"

"I guess. All at once. One spree or over some time?"

"All within a year. By the time of my birthday, my ninth, he was in jail. He's the librarian at the jail now."

"It happens."

"You know it. The third murderer, if you want to know, and I know you do, everyone does, was a state trooper who killed his wife. Kitchen knife. But first he choked her, so hard, he broke one of the little bones in her neck, then when she was still alive, they say, he slit her throat. They had adopted twins, her sister's boys who weren't at home. My mom says there are blessings in everything if we have the sense to find them. Damon and James not being at home—that's a big one."

"That's pretty decent. As a killing. It will be hard to get back to my risk management thing after talking to you. Hell, I wanted a GED anyway. Cooler. Do you have a diploma or a GED?"

"No, I went all the way. The whole deal, graduation parties, a car for a present. I even got the extra certificate in computers, so I can run an office. I mean if I wanted to which I do not. I want to set up my own salon. Nails, hair, skin."

"That sounds cooler than sitting in front of a screen all day. Did the trooper go to jail and run the infirmary or laundry?"

"No, his trial is dragging out. It's not a question about whether he did it. He called his neighbor with the knife still in his hand. He was yelling and crying, I don't believe the crying, do you? But he was yelling into the phone, 'I'm sorry.' The neighbor didn't know what was up, so went over, and found a big mess. All in the kitchen though. So, they didn't have too much trouble cleaning up and putting the house up for sale. It still hasn't moved, as they say, but that's because of the market, we think. His brother spoke at her funeral and his parents paraded themselves down to the front of the church, big as could be, as if they were at any funeral."

"You never know, do you, what people will do next."

"It's the truth."

"Number four, since you asked for it. It was set up to look like an intruder did it, but it turned out to be a man who had worked for the old lady. Old means forty-two. He thought she didn't pay him enough and that she had a bunch of money stashed away in her house, one of those new mansions that looks like it belongs in Europe or somewhere weird."

"Was he caught?" The boy is now sitting on the bench by the water fountain and trash can. He fishes out two dollar bills and points to the snack building, asking Regina if she wants a drink. She nods and follows him over and pushes the coke button. He gets one too. They walk back to the bench. It's cooling off now, Regina's favorite time of day when everything goes blurry, she calls it.

It's very nice to have someone new to tell these stories to. Everyone she knows knows them already, so they don't want to hear them. She sits down. He bends over his knees, his elbows propping him up, the red Coke can dangling in one hand as if it is too heavy to hold. It makes her want to help him hold it. She can see his scalp through his buzz cut and a tattoo of a snake there. She's never seen a scalp tattoo. Her mom says you can always learn something. Her purse is feeling heavy on her shoulder from the gun in it and she pulls it closer to her and can feel the metal warm up next to her stomach.

Honest Money

"No one could have made all this money honestly." She was on the front porch looking out at the wedding guests, over two hundred, the biggest wedding in the county, ever. Cars were parked up and down the highway for two miles, washed, waxed, glaring in the June sun. The white fences on both sides of the highway were the only ones in the county. It was, I would learn later, an effort to bring a little stretch of Kentucky horse country to Virginia. And later, in a low time, the bride ordered her tombstone engraved with "She Brought the Hunt to Southside," and when it came, kept it in the barn, but that was a long time after her wedding day, a long time of madness and what we learned to call "drama."

That day, my grandmother's favorite grandchild, Howard—everyone else called him Dab, short for Dabney, his middle name—had just married Irene, the richest girl he could find. Dab did not have our grandmother's problem with rich people. He loved everything about them: cars, houses, fences, horses, cattle, timber. My own parents had married for different reasons, just as farfetched. Mama had married daddy to make him happy, and he had married her to make her unhappy, not that either one of them understood what they were doing at the time. He thought he had been taken with the way Mama looked—a young woman who had played hockey in college and wore a green felt hat with a short feather in it. She thought he could be rescued from his family whose idea of letting a boy go outside and play was to tie him to the clothesline and let him run up and down it all afternoon, rain or shine.

I was twelve at Irene and Dab's wedding, helpless, agonized, and proud of grandma for speaking out to the guests who were used to her pronouncements and weren't listening. And, I was thrilled that Dab was marrying Irene whose family owned three thousand acres, a long beige Cadillac and lived in a big house with a two-story front porch, the one we were standing on, with drop down Mt. Vernon columns. We could see the grand piano through the tall windows.

It was too bad that what Grandma said about honest money got back to Irene right after the wedding and staked out the rest of our lives. Irene hated all of us from then on, but some of us, the needy ones who wanted to be rich but did not know we did, us, she took into her camp, her confidence, her circle. Me especially. I was a child soldier recruited to carry her message to Dab's family: she was not a bad person. She wanted me to add that it was Dab's family who were the bad ones. This message was too complicated for me to carry. I didn't know how to tell my camp of Latin teachers, debt-ridden failed farmers, Methodists what they should think when they could see with their own eyes what was what. Every time I tried to deliver this wooden horse, no surprise, I got killed at the gates for betraying the most sacred flame. Irene was bad by all the principles my family knew and by all the smaller rules. She used bad words, had bad thoughts, she harbored plans for revenge, held grudges, was filled with hatreds, and never forgot slights. She measured people by the money they had made on their own, not that she thought it was bad to have inherited it. In fact, she thought it was stupid if you did not inherit anything. She believed the very things that I had been taught were wrong. Absolutely.

Still, to be chosen by Irene, called every morning for years, before seven and laid out for some negligence not just from me but from, later on, from her own children who had not sent her a postcard from a weekend trip they'd made. Sometimes, she was furious with me that my family, Dab's worthless crowd, lived along the river, in a river house, while her family, better in every way, had land in the middle of the county, lined with the white fences, but miles away from the river. We had two hundred mortgaged acres, and she had, as I have said, three thousand, the beige Cadillac, horses, tracks of timber in counties sixty miles away—everything. Plus, she had won a blue ribbon at The Garden. It was gauche she taught me, to say Madison Square Garden. I was only Flo to her Irene, a real name, not a nickname.

Later when things got really bad, Irene and Dab's youngest daughter, Aster, burst out crying in the dark yard as she walked with me to my car parked after one of Irene and Dab's parties, that Irene had been "leaving bruises" on Dab. She called them Irene and Dab. Aster was thirteen then, a year older than I had been at her parents' wedding. I was home from my first divorce, exactly twice as old as Aster. I had been her babysitter and knew how she would go silent, even at four, and not talk for a week. Irene said she didn't blame Aster, and that she would do the same if she could, but everything would go to hell if she shut down. Her children were known for their wildness, "freedom," she called it. She let Aster play up in the attic with lighted candles. It helped her get through one of her silences, Irene said.

Grandma had worn her good church dress to the wedding, the one she would be buried in so she wore it only for special occasions, and this wedding was like a funeral so she did not mind the wear and tear it was getting in the heat. She hated weddings, watching lambs go to slaughter, but this one she said was worse than terrible. She dismissed the acres and the horses. We had a piano, one whose keys hit the velvet pads with a soft, cat-like pause between the notes that shrieked. When I complained, she told me that Albert Schweitzer had used a board to practice on. Later I would learn, too late, what I could have said, "Good for him."

Good voile can stand the heat. It was 1956 in central Virginia.

The wedding was in the small Baptist church that looked like a Greek temple. Irene's parents had given the land and the money to build the church and cemetery. We couldn't all get in the church and those who did almost fainted from the heat, ninety-eight degrees that afternoon. The bridesmaids looked about ready to die in their lavender organza ballerina-length dresses. Their faces were almost lavender under their matte makeup. No one had heard of air conditioning or big ceiling fans in 1956. Heat was natural. We understood the world.

Irene was known for her tantrums—from first grade through college. Dab knew about them. They were impressive, and he liked being impressed. When things went wrong, she threw a fit, and then things got better. I tried it once or twice at home with my parents and brother Eddie "to no avail." I loved that phrase and used it often. Tantrums didn't register at home.

Irene had thrown a big fit, we heard, when she told her parents that she was marrying Dab Peyton, Howard Dabney Peyton, my cousin. "Good luck" they'd said, then went on to warn her that she'd have to take care of him all his life which she did, running his life or trying to with her tantrums and her money which was really land that no one wanted to buy in our county. Still, Irene had the bearing, the "carriage" she said of a woman who owned many farms, who had won ribbons at horse shows, even at The Garden when she was eighteen. She understood money and we did not. She said she'd go to college after she got married, drive fifty miles every day, round trip, to take classes, and have three babies. This was her plan. She had a Phoenician profile and crinkling hair that she couldn't control, but in an age of flat haired page boys, she won my heart by swearing that she hated pageboys. On the night of the county beauty pageant, she had baled hay and then bathed and dressed for the pageant, her sunburn making her shoulders beautiful. I hated pageboys too, but as she said, I didn't have sense enough to know it, much less say it. My hair did not crinkle, it bent. I helped her with the two, not three, babies who could ride when they were three and were showing horses, hunter jumpers, at five. Aster started hunting on a stallion when she was six, getting special permission from the master of the hunt.

In his mid-seventies, after a life of hard drinking that kept his law practice inefficient and poor, Dab stopped drinking because of Irene's major tantrum which she called an intervention—one that brought her a small stroke and then death two years later. She blamed Dab for the stroke and held the sagging left side of her face against him, pointing to it and saying she owed her ruined beauty to him. Then, she'd point to Dab, who'd throw his arm around her shoulder and say to whoever was hearing the story, "But look at this other side. It's perfect. "She blamed her children, especially Aster, who went along with her, taking full credit for the plot, but somehow got her in the car and to the hospital.

I was Irene's friend, even at twelve, when she married Dab, and after that I was claimed as her cousin, or as mama said, her whipping post. Being five years older, Irene did not worry that I would not understand what she told me about her life with Dab and later about her sessions with her doctor; she was sure I couldn't, being who I was, part of Dab's family, but I would have to do, she said. I was all she had to work with as a friend. She wanted me to understand that she'd wanted to marry Dab, period. Forget the fact that he had about five girlfriends at the time, two of them putter-outers and several during their long marriage. Once I saw Dab in his own house at a Christmas party pushing a married woman—plump, glasses, permed hair—up against a wall and kissing her down her neck while she tried or seemed to try pushing him off her. Forget the fact that he was poor and worst of all, didn't mind it and never made any real money and screwed up the one case that would have moved him to the big time, that is, to Richmond money.

Our family, I was learning and not just from Irene, ruined the people we married, so Irene was a good test case: how much more could we ruin her? How would we know what we'd done and what had already been done? She said for years that Dab's (and my) grandmother had started the devastation at the wedding as she stood on the porch and spoke to the crowd like a Roman emperor to the crowd watching Christians being eaten by lions, a favorite scene in "Quo Vadis" with us, about no honest person could have paid for such a wedding. But later, Irene found out that Grandma had only been a small part of her problem and to her credit, she acknowledged that it was her own father who had ruined her. This fact took years to discover and more years to adjust to, but she never thought that he was dishonest about money, and she never forgave Grandma or any of Dab's family. And she'd add, even if her father had ruined her, he'd loved her, and that was more than we had done. No, she said, we hated her. All of us. She did not let us off the hook. It was true that Grandma thought money made people dishonest and Irene thought that smart good people made money. These two ways of thinking about money crashed into each other, and the crash started at the wedding even though it had started long before that.

I had not set my rifle sites on my first husband. I was learning a great deal at Irene and Dab's wedding that hot afternoon, not that I realized what was happening to its full extent. To me, back then, it was a perfect afternoon, and I was a helpless dangling puppet girl, hanging pigeon-toed in the hot sun. Irene was perfectly wrong for Dab, but she looked beautiful in her Montaldo's gown, as plain in its ivory sleeves that came down to points over her hands that were hard as leather gloves from holding the reins of her blue ribbon winning horses. I couldn't see the wrongness of things then, but Grandma always could. She and Irene had that in common. I had to learn the hard way.

Our family had never had any money, and Irene pointed out to me three months after the wedding, we never would have any, the way we carried on about the starving Armenians and Korean orphans. We thought we still lived in a big house handing out corn bread and sacks of flour, giving the ex-slaves' great-grandchildren sides of bacon. In fact, Grandma did live in a ten room house, but the back porch was falling away, the screens billowed out of it, the broken milk separator stood guard by the door. Grandma wouldn't have curtains or rugs, reminding us that some people didn't have roofs. She said "rooves" not "rufs" the way our fifth-grade teacher had corrected me, but I kept loyal to "rooves." Her house had a heating system—heat registers cut in the ceilings above the wood stoves in the dining room and living room so that the heat rose up in waves and ribbons to the frozen bedrooms through iron grids. When she shook hands with a person she would report later how hard the person worked. Soft hands meant a person didn't work.

Irene's Five Year Plan

The day before she died, Irene called Ron who was in the hospital. He had just been moved from the ICU to the fifth floor, the Heart Wing, his name for the cardiac unit. Improving, the doctors said. But not really.

"I don't want to go to anybody's funeral. You hear me?" Irene was great on the telephone and she knew that Ron loved her calls. She kept him going he said to everyone. "Not many women you can say that about. "Knowing when to hang up was another one of Irene's telephone virtues, one hardly anyone else had. She was getting into texting, but her friends and family were still telephone people.

Ron smiled over the phone to hear Irene warn him about having a funeral she did not want to go to. They both felt better. She told him she liked his name for the cardiac unit. "Heart Wing is so much better!"

She could be sexy too and give a man a charge, even when he was in the hospital and even when she was on her death bed, but did not know it of course. She thought she had five more years. When Ron asked her how she felt, she'd answer in a darker whisper, "I feel good," and he knew he was supposed to say he was coming to see her and see how she felt for himself. It was their dirty talk, church rinsed, but very helpful to both of them, dulling their ache of loneliness, for different reasons, a procession of aches really, but never named separately.

She was a wreck herself—cancer—but because she was only three years into her five-year plan, she felt pretty good about things. Aster, the daughter she and Dab had had when they were forty, who would turn fourteen in a month, was finishing up her home school term, doing it mostly by herself with the help of the laptop Dab had bought on time for her. Irene knew that Aster used the answer book to get through the lessons, but so what, she was learning all the stuff. They had some tin-roof horse shows coming up, and the state horse show in August, would be a big deal. The house of new chickens would have been sent to market by August, and Dab could pay for the motel they would stay in for the show and take them out to the steak house every night. Dab was extravagant for a poor man on the verge of bankruptcy. He had bought a tandem bicycle for Irene and him, a "symbol" he called it, a word he had not used since senior English class in high school. "Of the future." Irene would go into remission and they would ride their country roads together, Dab doing the hard pedaling.

Things were good. It was too bad that Brenda, the foster child they'd taken in so Aster and Zoe would have a friend close at hand, had not worked out, and they missed the monthly check from social services. It had been too much—Brenda's gluten allergy, a bad fall down the basement steps. Things happen. The main thing was to see each day as a gift. Irene strung her days like pearls for Aster and Zoe and also for Dab.

The five-year plan meant that Aster's horses grazed in the front yard, forget the manure. It helped the grass. Irene's five-year plan called for many outings and treats for the four of them. Forget the credit card problems. Brenda had been part of the plan, but Irene was flexible and refused to see losing their eligibility for keeping her as a serious setback. The church groups had worn themselves out bringing meals, but that was fine too. Everything was good. It had to be. Dab had taken them to Luray Caverns and the home of James Madison. Day trips. Everything helped. The dogs helped too.

Irene knew that she was called the Dog Woman because she took in strays. She didn't mind because it was true, though she was sad that her beautiful name Irene went unused, wasted, when it could have been floating in all the conversations in the county. Irene's dogs and how many she had, up to nineteen now. Pastor Wong, the new minister at Hillcrest Methodist, did the same for people—took in strays and misfits—so he appreciated Irene, not just because of his deep South Korean Christianity that he had brought to Hillcrest, Virginia. It was more than that.

He came to visit Irene every week even though he was allergic to dogs. The first visit was just after he heard that she had walked out of the Baptist Church where she and Dab had been married in the middle of the sermon when the preacher said that while children were starving some people were feeding stray dogs. Dogs, the preacher had said, would be better off dead, and maybe the children would soon be too because they hadn't got the money that was being spent on dog food. The collection plate was going around at that point for the Children of the World Fund.

It was exactly at that point, evidently, that Irene, Aster, Zoe and Dab had stood up and walked out. Middle of the sermon. In fact, they had driven straight to Hillcrest

Methodist and come in just as Pastor Wong's sermon was coming to a soft landing. He was telling about his mother's prayer when there was no food in her house for the six of them back "in our village in South Korea." His mother had asked her children to sing a hymn, which they did, because as Pastor Wong explained, Korean children mind their mothers. The quavering, hungry little voices were heard by a missionary who was passing through their village. "Missionary stopped. Good Christian Man. Saved Us. Both Ways—Food and Spirit. Took all us to his mission center. We called him 'Angel Man.' We all worked there at the center until we left to come here, to America, many years later." Pastor Wong then broke into a grown man's version of the hymn he and his brother and sisters had sung that day. His voice was good enough for *American Idol* everyone said if the program took hymn singers.

No one had ever walked out of Mount Zion Baptist Church until that day. Mount Zion preached straight from the Bible, not like the Methodists who brought politics and issues to the pulpit. The month before Irene, Aster, Zoe and Dab appeared at Hillcrest Methodist, all the veterans—there were five—had walked out in a procession because Edith Taliaferro had put the American flag in the closet. Something about Iraq, Irene had heard. Edith had not asked anyone about doing it and when she was asked why she did it, she said that the church was supposed to be a sanctuary from politics. The WWII vets had never heard such a thing. They said they thought Hillcrest Methodist was for Americans, "Or used to be," they had said. So they had walked out during Joys and Concerns. Pastor Wong was very happy to have Irene, Dab and their two girls march into the church mid-sermon. Now Joys and Concerns was Irene's favorite part of the service. Her name was frequently mentioned, and the way Pastor Wong said it made it sound even more beautiful than it already was. A hesitation, the "I" part, then a "L"ene.

Pastor Wong had come to tell Irene on Monday, that he welcomed Dab, Aster and Zoe with her at Hillcrest Methodist. He heard about her Five-Year Plan. Taking in stray dogs was one part of the plan. People left dogs to starve on the side of the road or to run off with the packs of wild dogs and she could hear barking at night deep in the woods. When word had spread about her taking in the dogs, people started bringing baskets of puppies leaving them on her porch. She refused to give up the three oldest dogs —they couldn't walk any better than she could on her bad days. She told Pastor Wong about the thunderstorm that had brought in one dog so frightened that he had knocked open their front door, found her and Dab in bed and had jumped in with them. She told him about Ron in the Heart Wing, and he went to see him both at the hospital and after he came home, the day after he conducted the funeral service for Irene.

A Breath Away

We needed green stain for the kitchen cabinets, so on my way home from work, if you can call what I do work, answering the phone for Costner's Insurance Agency, I went by Baer's Hardware. I say we needed the green stain when the truth was that I needed to do something, anything, and the kitchen was as good a place as any for me to offer myself some help. Nell Gilliam had given me this bad advice for what she calls "the problem with Harry" as if she did not have her own set of problems with Richard, but anyway, her advice was to take on a project like the kitchen cabinets. And, I admit I need help and am glad to have any that is available. As the old song says, "Help, help me, Rhonda."

I am living alone as I have been for fifteen years, but I still think as a we, that Harry still lives at home with me, that we are married in the ordinary sense of things. Our kitchen cabinets would be so much better green, everything would seem better with a green kitchen. That's how Nell Gilliam wants me to think. It is clear to me that she concentrates on my problems with Harry to avoid hers with Richard. I know I am repeating myself.

I write out my return address on letters and bills Mrs. Harry W. Lassiter, not Ms. Joyce M. Lassiter, and I never will. I know what people say about Harry and me. That I am in denial and that Harry has lost his mind and thinks with his penis. I agree somewhat with the Harry part but not the part about me. I know how much I can stand and feel that every test makes me stronger. The Lord does not give us more than we can stand, though sometimes, I think He underestimates the weight of things we bear like when I almost signed the divorce papers when Harry came crying to me saying that Estelle had accused him of poisoning her. You should have done just that I said to him as he sat at our kitchen table, his head down on his arms, crying like a baby. He pretended he didn't hear me and went on talking down to the table wet with his tears that our divorce was the only thing that would help him. Then he went on with the poisoning story. The sheriff, our old friend, Wayne, had been smiling, Harry said, and had only come out to Harry's when Estelle called him because he was worried that Estelle might hurt Harry, but Wayne's smiling in his uniform only made Estelle madder, so mad she ran out the house and took herself and their baby, who, poor thing, has turned out to be retarded—we can tell now that Malcolm is five—to a shelter for abused women. Somehow, I held out and kissed Harry and told him I could not give him a divorce, a divorce was not what he needed. He needed to come back home. I added that he would never get a divorce from me. Nell thinks I should kick Harry out of my life. I say to her in my head that she should go first and jump out the airplane.

Baer's Hardware had the green stain I needed. The old fashioned store was in its last stages of life because the Walmart Super Center had moved just outside Moneta twelve years ago. Somehow Baer's was staying in business. When I walked in, the man at the counter in a big black cowboy hat caught me in his wide-lens salesman's smile bringing me closer to him. Why he wasn't embarrassed by the hat I should have guessed, and it made a kind of sense after we got through talking about what paint or stain would cover the layers of grease and Liquid Gold and Murphy Oil buildup on my cabinets.

The hat was my problem, not his. I had come that far in my own kind of therapy: the way I see the world is my way/my world. The world wobbles and shifts depending on who's doing the seeing or talking. This is a very old insight that I am just now getting my head around, as our daughters say to me.

The cowboy's wife Jeanne had been dead a year this past December second, he told me when we were a few minutes past talking about staining the cabinets. It turned out that I had known Jeanne years ago, and, in fact, I had heard that Jeanne had died, but had forgotten. She had been such a pretty girl, the prettiest in our high school class. He nodded mildly at my attempts at belated sympathy, taking them for what they were worth. Then, he began his story, even though he wished I were a better person to hear it, I could tell. It registered that he had not gotten a note or even a sympathy card from a Mrs. Harry Lassiter because I never sign my name Mrs. Joyce Lassiter, as I said, the way divorced women do. His Christianity impelled him to forgive me and to reach out to me, so I had to stand there and be forgiven and reached. It wasn't as bad as it sounds. I don't think I would try telling Nell to reach out for Richard in a Christian or any kind of way. I say she needs to hit him with an axe. We are violent about each other's husbands. Nell can freeze your heart with a look, but I may try to get through to her.

The cowboy could settle the problem of my cabinets. He had just the thing, called, he said, without a smile,

"Greased Lightning." The cabinets needed some of that "product" before they could be stained, even with the deep poison green I thought would hide all the streaks and scars.

That little discussion out of the way, he started his story, getting my permission the way people always do. One look, and they are off. The day Jeanne died, they had made cookies all day for the nursing home people they knew. In the afternoon, Jeanne had sat down and said, "Len, I feel a little pain, right here."

Len pointed to his chest and explained to me, "Her heart. She felt a little pain in her heart. That's all she said, though, 'a little pain,' and then she was gone."

"I am so sorry." I repeated it twice, but sorrow like the cowboy hat was my problem. He was the one who had dealt with losing Jeanne and had put it, if not behind him, then where it belonged and could be useful not only to himself but to others. Useful to me, this woman who thinks what she needs is green stain. I could see him thinking this about me. He had been heart-broken since that moment two years ago when Jeanne had felt her little pain, but had drawn a Christian message from the sad story, and would be glad to draw it for me. I dreaded the message coming from this Lash LaRue-Tex Ritter-Roy Rogers in a black hat behind the counter the way I dread anyone who tries to tell me something for my own good like get rid of Harry or asks me how long it's going to take me to wake up. I dread Nell's opinions about Harry, but since Richard has gone around the bend, not that Nell admits it, she is more careful about handing out advice to me.

"We are only a breath away, you know. But, the good news is that Jeanne is," at this point, he pointed with his heart finger to the heating ducts in the store, "waiting for us up there, waiting for that happy time when we will join her and be together forever."

He seemed aware that his last two words rhymed as if he were performing a country song, and of course, he had told this story, sung this song many times in the last two years. In fact, he was saying, he had written Jeanne's story into a song and performed it at the nursing home and at church suppers around town. He was honoring me, he said sweetly, by telling me his story and about his plan to reunite with Jeanne.

He had faith that the story would be useful to me, maybe not in ways I could see at first, or ever, but he felt sure that I might be able to pass on what he had learned and do some good somewhere. I might not remember, he said, that Jeanne had the shiniest brown hair to go perfectly with her shiny brown eyes. I said I did remember, and added that the girls had all been a little jealous. He nodded, of course, they had been.

Years ago when she had come to my high school as a senior, Jeanne had been pretty, very pretty, so pretty that one long-time teacher's marriage had almost hit the rocks, and one of the coaches almost got divorced from his wife for making a fool of himself over a girl who was not doing anything but being seventeen, throwing her whole self into a laugh, twirling around corners instead of just walking, making it the fashion to roll up the cuffs of her short sleeved blouses and put the back of her collar up like the boys did.

Turning herself and flipping her hair a lot for all of us to admire. Nell wasn't there. She moved here later with Richard, but if she had been, she would have seen what there was to see in Jeanne.

The Coach's wife had told her friends who told me years later that Jeanne, "that little piece," had brought her and the Coach "to the brink," and that she had been just a hair away from leaving him. One night she had packed up the children and put them in the car and there they sat in the cold out in the yard for three hours. She had made sandwiches and taken a thermos of hot chocolate and chips so the kids thought they were going on a long trip. She had games for them to play and she read to them. She gave the Coach until five o'clock—it was around two when she got everything in the car—to set things straight with Jeanne, whatever that meant. It was late November, raining, dark, Christmas was coming, she even had the turkey and ham in the freezer, but she was ready to leave if the coach didn't get rid of Jeanne to whatever degree they were involved. She was generous to give him three hours to decide. That's how hard hearted she was, how hard hearted Nell thinks I should be with Harry and how I think she should be with Richard. I've given Harry years to make up his mind and when he does, if I don't like his decision, I go along my way, ignoring what he's decided. The Coach's wife could have just left. At four fifty-two, she said the Coach (she called him Coach evidently) got it straight and came out to the car and told them to come back in the house. The children did not seem to mind sitting out in the car and having a picnic in the cold. They must have been the true children of the Coach, tough, obedient, careless of discomfort and arbitrary rules and defensive strategies. She had kept starting the engine to run the heater.

Jeanne did not go to college, didn't need to go because she was so pretty. Being almost that pretty, I went for two years. I had not seen Jeanne or heard how her life turned out, and I was surprised that Jeanne's widower was this mild man who worked in her parents' hardware store and wore a cowboy hat, a man who had not been surprised that she had been just a breath away from eternity as she baked cookies for the nursing home. That's what we all are, he repeated, whether we know it or not.

Later, the Greased Lightning and the green stain turned out to be wrong, the cabinets needed to have polyurethane to finish them off and to give them a little glow. When I went back to Baer's, Len said he thought that I knew that. "Everyone knows about polyurethane." I needed to go over the green cabinets with two coats. He had been sure that I knew that much about redoing kitchen cabinets. I got an apology from Len who smiled and said he certainly should have told me but repeated that he thought I would know that cabinets needed those finishing coats, the protection factor, or that I had friends who would have known and told me. Then he launched into another story from his life with Jeanne.

It was a set-up, a trap to get a listener. I might as well have been one of the nursing home people, parked in a wheel chair, listening to his songs and story about Jeanne. I was sure that he had not told me about the polyurethane for the cabinets so I would have to come back to the store, and then he could tell me another chapter in his book of love. He actually used that old song title. Sometimes, I am sure that Nell sets me up, traps me to tell me her stories and to make noises about my stories about Harry.

Like everyone, he began, Jeanne had been under a lot of stress, so it was not really hard to believe when he looked back on it that she had had that little pain in her heart and had gone so quickly. She had a heart murmur, and yes, of course, they knew about it. She had arrhythmia. They knew that all along.

I wanted to yell into his sweet smile that some of us have a big pain there where he kept pointing to, just to the left of his bola tie. I wanted to tell him that Harry, who hasn't lived at home for almost fifteen years, is—there is no other word for it—dating me. Not that we are going steady. He came by last week, Tuesday, stood outside talking about his radiation treatments, and when he was getting in his truck to leave, he had said "You know, Joyce, I love you." Fool that I am, I murmured, just as if we were on a date, and just as if he had not been heading back to Estelle and the house they have bought and have been living in with their retarded boy Malcolm, "I know, Harry." Just as if I haven't heard through the grapevine that Harry brags that Estelle has the flattest stomach in the state of Virginia. And, he and I both know that when he was a boy, he said he couldn't date me because I wasn't pretty enough. When I heard that I went off to college for two years, but I guess he changed his mind, and then changed it back, and now, I guess I am pretty enough to date anyway. I always put on lipstick in the morning and an ironed blouse. It's old fashioned, but it's me. Nell thinks it's crazy and that I am crazy and that Harry is happy as a king.

What could Mr. Christian Cowboy say to the level of stress I live under?

But this chapter of his Jeanne story was called "Embezzlement." He himself called it "this chapter" and began. Jeanne had suspected something for years about the store, and then had laid a trap, the paper work, which means these days, he explained, computer files, and caught their old friend, Laura Norris, red handed, her hand in the till, changing the amounts on the bank deposits and pocketing the difference. Over the years, Laura had done very well with this extra income. She had put that new kind of siding on her house, replaced the carpeting and wiring, put in a new heat pump, paid off her credit cards and gotten a new Taurus. At first, Jeanne had blamed the Walmart Super Center for the slow drain on Baer's, but when she had studied the computer files, she could see what had happened, brilliantly done with no discernable pattern of discrepancy, a different amount every month, and not every month. Not discernable, Len said sadly and proudly, to anyone else until Jeanne had put her mind to it, and come to the terrible conclusion that it was Laura who was stealing from Baer's. It had been too much, and it had killed Jeanne.

Now Laura Norris was serving a nine-year sentence for almost ruining Baer's Hardware, but not for the real crime of murder. She had been much worse than the Walmart for all of them. A murderer.

"You could say that Laura Norris killed my Jeanne. In fact, I do say it. Rather, I sing it in my songs."

I agreed with Len. I could see where he was coming from. I could say that Estelle was killing me, slowly, like the embezzler, Laura Norris, had killed Len's Jeanne. I don't blame Harry like Nell thinks I should. I blame Estelle. I am familiar with the killer, much more familiar with her than Jeanne was with Laura Norris. Some people would say that I am dating my killer but I don't. They tell me about women who are killed by their boyfriends and husbands. Those are their favorite television shows. Nell once said that I was lucky with my problem because it was so obviously a problem. She meant that with Richard she never knew what was going on. He would just try to kill himself every now and then.

But, I have loved Harry since I first saw him, and I have been married to him for forty-three years if you count all the years and not just the ones that he lived at home. We have two almost perfect sons, a nice brick ranch house, and an asphalt driveway up to the two-car garage, a life that is the same life we used to live in many ways, except now he lives with Estelle and dates me. He used to live with me and date Estelle. A traditional adultery. No one understands this new dating, but everyone is used to it. Even Estelle, I hear, has stopped having fits that send her to the emergency room with panic attacks and migraines which I hear, from Harry, are so bad they come close to setting off mini-strokes. I tell Harry that I have had shingles twice because of our situation. He wants my sympathy for Estelle's visits to the emergency room, but he thinks that I can deal with shingles and anything else that comes along. He just smiles his teenaged heart-throb smile and I go on listening on our date. Nell and Richard live in rented places, have a big mortgage on a house they can't live in because he can't keep a job there, so he goes off to wherever he can land a job and Nell stays at home, mostly, though she has gone as far as North Carolina.

I know that I am my own worst enemy in small ways, not just with Harry. I wash paper plates, wash the dishes before I put them in the dishwasher, and buy cakes at Sam's but then make boiled chocolate icing for them. I save money as I waste it. The same with my life. I date a killer as the television would say. I have heard stories about Nell and Richard's marriage, their living apart, him in Georgia, her in North Carolina, then their move back to Virginia. I don't have much sympathy for them. They are the ones deciding what's what. I don't get to decide when Harry comes and goes. They must make some of their crazy decisions together. I get to decide on the green stain for the kitchen cabinets.

Len was talking about his Jeanne's last moment over the cookie sheet. He was certain that she had been thinking about Laura Norris' stealing from the store for years. She was only a breath away from eternity, and if she had known that, she might have thought of something different and not about Laura Norris. She might have recalled her girlhood or maybe even one of her first dates with him when he had been so happy, he'd almost wrecked his dad's '68 Chevy Nova.

Once when Harry and Estelle were away at Myrtle Beach for a week—Harry said they needed to get away—I tried to feel divorced, the way our children want me to practice feeling, to get some relief, but it did not work. When they got back from the beach, I called Harry to ask him to come to a lacrosse game—our little nine-year-old grandson is a star on his team and plays early on Saturday mornings. It would be cool and it would give Harry a break from Estelle after being cooped up with her at the beach. I still think of what Harry needs, and we will talk about what he needs when he takes me to lunch in Richmond and then sends me flowers. That's when I do feel a breath away from my real life, and not from eternity, but close to my real life here on earth. Nell can think what she pleases, but I bet she'd like to have a date with Richard and carve out a little happiness here.

Wyoming

Two days after Richard left to drive to Georgia—it's a ten-hour drive from my apartment here in Newnan, North Carolina, to his in Tifton, Georgia—he came back. Because I don't have a clock by my bed, I did not know what time it was when he walked in. Later I realized that it must have been around two-thirty.

August nights are not all that dark in North Carolina. Not as dark as they are in Virginia where we have our real home. Here in North Carolina, I can walk around in my apartment without turning on a lamp—so when Richard sat on the edge of my bed in the filtered gray early morning that Tuesday, I could see him almost as plainly as I would five hours later when I made coffee for us. He had talked as we sat crouched on the bed, if you can call saying "I don't know" between silent stretches, talking. And, I was not listening. Oh, I was trying to, and I don't know even now what to call what I was doing as Richard talked except going crazy—walking down steps in my head, in that half-darkness where I could and couldn't see and could and couldn't feel the steps under my feet. This could-and-couldn't-see-and-feel is the way I see things now. I know that I am walking, but it feels as if I am climbing over a fence the way I did as a girl, only now I'm not running across the field on the other side of the fence as I did then.

Mental illness, like love or happiness, must be different for everyone, its onset dependent on the person and the situation, and that morning, when I had what I now call my mental breakdown, I turned into an efficiency expert, one who could have clients, arrange conferences for scientists from all over the world, keep data banks—anything. I could do anything, but on the other hand, I couldn't keep my husband alive. I was going down steps in the dark at the same time that I was making complicated plans for our future lives, while he was not wanting to be alive.

I already had several areas of expertise but of an old-fashioned useless kind—I could clean and dress a deer, packaging it in dinner-sized roasts, the zip-lock bags stacked in the freezer, I could knit (a straight stretch for the back of a sweater or a length of scarf) or nurse a baby while driving, and I have one or two other talents that are modern perversions of frontier skills. The things I could do very well, the sad thing was, no one needed doing and none of them would have helped or had, I was beginning to see that August night, helped Richard or me.

At nine that morning, when I should have been making calls to the rescue squad or the hospital, I called the mortgage company's branch office to ask if we could borrow another sixty thousand dollars, if we could take a third mortgage out on our home back in Virginia. It was Colonial Credit's Carol Mahoney, a person I knew only on the phone as our credit counselor, who got the first call and my first version of Richard's suicide attempts.

My conversation with Ms. Mahoney omitted the key "s" word and emphasized "attempts" as in the ones we had made to reduce our debts. I let her think what was natural for her to think. I was another client in trouble with money.

That was also true. She was pleasant and encouraged us to come in around ten for an evaluation of our situation, and to bring our last year's tax returns and all our credit cards. It did not matter that we were talking refinancing in North Carolina about property in Virginia. She laughed a little and said money matters were like McDonald's, the same everywhere, and they had a new program called "The Fence" which was designed to contain a certain area of debt that threatened to get out of hand. I had thought that our living in two states would be a problem, and owning a mortgaged home in a third another, but I was wrong. No one minded.

At first when Richard had leaned toward me in the semi-dark and put his hand on my shoulder, I turned toward him and could see that his face looked different, shaken loose from the bones and then carelessly draped back. I thought that I was dreaming my old dream: Richard was at home; we were living together again. This, we had joked for seven years, was our impossible dream. Living together. It would never happen, but in that after midnight darkness in North Carolina, it seemed to me that I had been awarded my last wish by some foundation like the one that takes dying children to Disney World. Richard was back at home. We were both at home. A miracle.

I had been asleep facing the wall, my back to the door, and even in the unairconditioned upstairs apartment, I was covered up with the old eiderdown comforter.

"I'm sick," were Richard's first words, then he took his hand away as if my shoulder were burning, too hot to touch. I got my elbows under me and said his name, and then sat up to see him turning away, bending over and putting his head down as if he were going to faint or vomit beside the bed. After I shook off that first silken-dream feeling that a miracle had happened and that an apparition that looked like Richard had come to announce it, I began to think of his cluster headaches, the migraines. These must have hit him, but he had somehow managed to drive back to me in my North Carolina apartment to take his medicine, the Imitrex along with the Fironel. Maybe he had forgotten his bag of medicine. Maybe he was planning to sleep the attack off in my apartment with me standing by with ice packs. Sometimes I try the hot water treatment which works just as well as the ice. A pan of hot water, as hot as his feet can stand it—the blood vessel walls expand, the blood leaves the head, flows to his feet in the pan, and voila, the headache evaporates. I had many homeopathic cures for Richard, ones that seemed to me to work as well as the medicines and the oxygen tank by the bed. Oxygen expands the blood vessels in the brain: headache vanishes. Same as with the feet in the hot water but requires more equipment and costs more. We had not seen about getting an oxygen tank for North Carolina or Georgia and had let the rental agreement run out in Virginia.

Headaches made sense to me briefly, replacing the miracle thing. A headache had brought Richard home.

Now I have come to know that an ordinary explanation, as ordinary as headaches and forgotten medicines, are the real miracles. Nothing, I should have known but didn't, could have been further from the truth than headaches, or forgotten medicine, or fatigue—those old friends.

Too much time—two long days—had passed since Richard had driven his loaded car off from me in North Carolina toward Georgia. In two days he should have gotten there—to Tifton where he could have taken his medicine—he keeps an extra supply in his apartment, he could have called his office to say that he was not coming in to work, and he could have slept off the Fironel in his Tifton apartment without me, without my ice packs or foot pans of hot water. Then it flashed across my mind that maybe he had quit his new job, maybe he did not have an office to call, and had come back to me, or worst of all, maybe he had been fired again.

There had been problems in Tifton—three people had suddenly resigned from his assessment strategies team. There had been a scandal in the older faculty and then, unbelievably, the murder of the young popular English teacher, the wife and mother, the star of the small department. The perfect couple, the ones who headed two departments and were given awards at graduation. And worst of all, the murderer turned out to be the perfect husband who for the three weeks after the murder had been in everyone's mind the grieving victim of random violence—the grieving widower. He had used their kitchen knife.

My thoughts were louder than Richard's words, drowning them in a heavy surf which was one reason I could not understand him, could not hear what he was saying about trying and making attempts, choosing the trees and bridges for the past seven years, he didn't know how long, maybe longer. I was caught, snagged, on the murder story in Georgia. I knew that Richard had been trying to help the husband with all the paperwork he had to do for the accreditation of his department. And I knew that the slashed-to-death wife, the young woman who had read Richard's poems to her class in modern poetry, had appreciated his help. Richard had gone to see the grieving husband in those first days before he had been arrested, before there was the least suspicion. This was the father who that day had waited for his children to be picked up to play with friends, and then after he had seen them off, as his wife got ready to go shopping, had killed her when she walked into the kitchen. Then he had called 911 to report that he had found her murdered.

The husband did not even have to say "intruder," because that was so obvious. I had sent flowers to her funeral from Richard and me, a funeral which had to be held at the college's gym because of the huge crowd. This murder was part of Richard's life in Tifton, Georgia.

Slowly, the fact, the "s" word, made its way to me through Richard's "I don't knows," through all of the pictures in my head of the killer husband and dying wife, her funeral, the children taken away to the grandparents, the arrest, the community's shock. Not that I had heard Richard use the word "kill. "But I was thinking so hard about the murdered young woman. She had been killed. Kill was the word connected to her. Someone else must be involved in a killing. Not Richard.

Two days is a long time, too long for the ten-hour drive from me in Newnan, North Carolina, to Richard's place in Tifton, Georgia. Two days is a long time in America to be out of touch with all our cell phones and emails.

And, there was Richard's smell. Something dangerous. His shirt was warm and oily. I could tell from reaching across the bed toward him and putting my hand on his arm that it was the same shirt that he had worn when he had driven away on Saturday, two eternity-stretching days ago.

Things began to shift around in my head, trying to settle: it was Tuesday, wasn't it? I could see in the plain gray light that Richard was not in Georgia where he had been working for the past eighteen months. Wasn't he right there with me in North Carolina, sitting lopsided on the bed and talking toward me crouched and strangling a pillow in the warm darkness.

"I've been trying to kill myself. I came back an hour ago, but you were asleep, and you didn't hear me come up the steps, so I left and tried again to drive the car into the Saluda River, or into one of the trees I'd chosen. Really, there were several trees, three bridges. I forget what other rivers. I think I lost count. I got as far as Statesville once, and to Charlotte, and then I drove west toward Asheville. Now I'm back here again. I couldn't do it. So I'm home, well, not really at home, but here at your apartment anyway. I've been driving for two days. I think it's been two. But I've been choosing trees for a long time. Two state cops have stopped me for drifting across the lines or toward the median, but they both let me off with a warning."

This was when I heard the word, but this was as clear as it got, except for the amount he had just mentioned, "over fifty thousand."

I was keeping my hand on the arm that did not feel like Richard's. He was speaking toward the floor.

"I can't go on, not any longer. I tried to do it when Nick was here the last time, so it would be easier for her. I was thinking that she wouldn't have to fly home again if I would go the hell ahead with it. I know that I'm not thinking right, but I thought that Vince could take it. And I knew you would be all right. I don't know. I've waited for them to grow up. Grown children get over things. And I was thinking with their new jobs they could help you pay off the fifty thousand.

By then, my head was beginning to split open, slowly the way some logs do after one blow from the axe. You can see and hear the crack run down the log though it does not fall open into halves but lies there on the ground, whole.

The day before, on Monday afternoon, I had walked across the clear cut field behind the old house where I am renting the upstairs from a Mrs. Juanita Morris. The land had been burnt over to prepare for planting pine seedlings, a cash crop for my landlady's grandchildren to harvest, a nice crop of trees, Juanita had said when I had asked about the stretch of what looked like wilderness. She had said she called the fields that rolled away from the house, Wyoming, but she meant no offence to that state. She'd never been to Wyoming, and now she never wanted to go. She was already there she explained, whether she wanted to be there or not. She was able to cross Wyoming off her list of places she wanted to visit before she died, and she added she knew that I might know what she and her husband were dealing with. She meant their grandchildren, the two who lived nearby and who kept her upset and praying hard.

A red fox had run across one of the knolls and a buzzard flew down so close that I could hear the wind in his feathers.

120

I had taken the fox running over the charred logs as a good omen for us—Richard in his job in Georgia, me in my apartment in North Carolina, my extra job as a tutor for fifth year students in a small private college that offers renewable teaching contracts, Nick and Vince in their first jobs after college—and when the buzzard swooped to within a hundred feet of me, I had felt as high as the thin clouds, happy to be dismissed by the buzzard as carrion! Passed over! And happy not to be seen by the fox picking its way carefully across the blackened logs and stumps, the tall green pokeberry stalks growing right beside them. I felt pride, crazy as it seemed, to have gone West, to have seen Wyoming. I did not know then, of course, on Monday afternoon, when I was walking under the buzzard's flight and out of sight of the fox that Richard was beginning his long drive. This was the month before 9/11. Now I divide all events into Before and After that day in August, as the families of World Trade Towers and the Pentagon victims do, as maybe everyone does now. For me, it's August the twentieth that divides time. I know that we are not victims in the terrible way that the Washington and New York families are and now all the families of soldiers are. And the Iraqis and Afghans. I know that.

I cried every night for a month after that, and then I stopped crying.

The next time Richard used pills, all the headache medicine he had saved. After that we went to doctors. I went to some of the sessions. Two years later, I had what passed for an answer, the one anyone could have told us, but we were paying the doctor to tell us.

Richard's perfect childhood, the grandfather who took him fishing, the clam bakes in New Hampshire, the peach ice cream, homemade on Sunday afternoons, all of these were, in fact, the slow torture of brain washing to make him know forever that he must not ever cause his perfect parents any trouble of any kind. They must never be disturbed by him. The enemas that the doctor said were, in fact, rapes, sodomizings, these were ways his mother used to control him, but in ways that were approved of, accepted, and presented with clean, heavy towels and warm water as ways to help his stomach pains.

He can remember running away from his mother, around and around the house, screaming until his throat gave out and she caught him. He never caused his mother any other trouble except running away from those humiliations in the bathroom. As he got older, she made him give the enemas to himself. The doctor sees a direct connection between these self-administered torments and the suicide attempts.

I say or said before the doctor helped us that Richard saved all the trouble in his life for us, long after his parents were dead. Or, as his doctor would say, he saved the trouble for himself and then did it to himself, but now I say that he came back to Wyoming.

What Matters

Sam was the cousin who was adopted, but it was Sam who was the happiest about the idea of a family reunion in July. The blood kin were not all that happy about getting together because we lived within an hour of each other, some of us closer. On a three-mile stretch along the James River, there were five families, some temporarily not speaking to each other, some who would never speak.

The summer before the reunion Sam had re-married, and maybe that's why he wanted a reunion to show off his new bride, not just in the emailed pictures. He brought us the album and a video of their wedding, not apologizing that he had emailed the same pictures earlier. The ceremony in the Grand Canyon, the helicopter taking Teresa and him with the minister down in a swirl of dust and noise and then returning to pick them up in the grandeur of rocks and clouds near the orange abyss.

Sam leased a white Yukon for the trip up from Florida to us in Virginia and rented four rooms at the motel because he said he knew that our house was "full up." We hoped it would be, though we did not trust our daughters to come home. We were right. They didn't. Lillie is now married to Daniel, and Clara has just divorced Bryan, but at the time of the reunion, Clara was planning a knockdown drag-out wedding for later in the summer.

Sam was not adopted in the usual sense of the word. In fact, he was the illegitimate son of his adopted father's nephew. So, he grew up as his real father's first cousin. Legal papers made the adoption seem like an ordinary one. The sown wild oats of that nephew, Sam's real dad, had been reaped, a version of the prodigal son, we said, and had landed the baby back where he belonged, almost. No one knew who Sam's mother was and no one cared. Some said it was just a good thing Sam was white. "How white?" one cousin asked. This was Irene, who prided herself on understanding the times.

Then she told the story we all knew about Bruce Lawson's daughter running off with a black man back when that meant something. "All the white men in the world to choose from, and plenty of them her kind of no good trash. No, she had to do something stupid like that, go off with, marry a black. Bruce told her if she did, she wouldn't get a cent of his money, which was a lot of money then, all the land plus the heavy equipment business, but she walked away with the two girls, into another world. My heart goes out to my friend Bruce. He tried to stop Teresa. She had a good husband, good enough, the second one who saw her through her computer training. It must have been drugs for her to walk away from all the money Bruce has. I'm surprised she took her girls with her, sweet little things who ran the house with their dad for her, and maybe she's counting on them, I bet, to do the same for the new man."

Irene by the time of the reunion was too sick to come, but she already knew what would happen she said so didn't have to bother to be there, and she outlined a few things that would happen after she died. She meant we would all be sorry we hadn't listened to her about what matters. What mattered, her big truth that summer, had to do with what love meant. "You don't have to be loved in order to love." That's what she tried to get us to understand, and she used herself as the big example, admitting that she was often unlovable, but she never stopped loving us and she never let go of us, which was essentially her definition of love—holding on even if you strangled the person or pulled him under the water. It was the reverse of what all the shrinks say, even the ones in the magazines in my doctors' offices. Her shrink had told her for the eighteen years, she said, that she understood what real love was. This wisdom had cost many thousands of dollars. She had five doctors for her pulmonary fibrosis, she would say, but just one doctor for her mind and soul.

Irene thought the Bible meant what she said it meant. She said she was paraphrasing Jesus so we could understand what He meant: you can love anybody if you set your mind to it, can stay married to anybody even. "Look at me" she'd say and laugh. She was married to a saint.

As a surprise for all of us, Sam had tee shirts made for the reunion. He wanted them to be given out as prizes—to the oldest, to the one who had come the farthest, to the one with the most grandchildren, and one for the most recently married, the rest he wanted us to sell, the money given to our church. Sam was sorry that his friend had printed the words backwards so that we could read what was written on them only if we looked in a mirror or wore them inside out. The shirts looked better anyway with the backwards writing of the name of the farm where we were having the deep pit barbecue: noinueR ylimaF weiV reviR.

That afternoon, there were other things to take in. Sam and his bride Teresa, their Grand Canyon wedding, weren't all we had to think about. There was McKenzie, the beautiful step-daughter of my cousin Tom with her illegitimate baby, a boy with long eyelashes who let us all take turns holding him. McKenzie did not know who the father was, and now she was dating a man in prison, if dating is the word to use for going to see someone behind bars. Her mother was also beautiful in an Indian way like McKenzie. It was Tom who brought McKenzie and the baby to the reunion and acted like the baby's dad, maybe because of McKenzie's mom's announcement that she loved the baby so much. She and Tom were in their mid-forties and not likely to start a second family—Tom had three from his first marriage.

At the reunion, it was Tom who was giving the baby his bottle and changing him while McKenzie sat around with Tom's family, the people her mother hated and so had refused to come to the reunion—all bored and beautiful, and with a lizard on her shoulder with a black velvet ribbon around its neck that she had tied to her wrist. She would ask us to pet the lizard and explain that it did not have teeth, "like a fish." I thought of sharks, but wasn't sure they were real fish, maybe mammals like I've heard whales are. I am "very limited" as my grandmother always said I was. The lizard was the color of molded cheese, and had a long tail that ran down McKenzie's arm. She stroked the lizard, and Tom played with her baby. I wondered what Irene would say about that when I told her. I was sure it wouldn't be anything close to what I felt.

Sam thought that he had come from nowhere, been found on a doorstep, and then brought to the Methodist orphanage in Richmond. His real father, the nephew of Sam's adopted father, had married ten years after Sam's adoption, a nurse, and they had had one child, a daughter, who was now an ophthalmologist, who, at forty, had not married. Sam's adopted parents, his aunt and uncle, were both dead, but his real father, the man he knew as his cousin was there with his wife. The ophthalmologist couldn't come. There were almost a hundred of us there for the reunion. Neighbors were invited too because they were always included in our big events. Vernon was there with Rachel, but not Vi. When we asked about Vi, he said she was at the hospital where she was a nurse, and had been called in for an extra shift. They were so proud of Vi's going through her training and never gave in to the fact that Vi hardly spoke to them. She drove a midnight blue BMW, and they were proud of that too. She had not explained her divorce, the one we had hoped would make her more understanding of unhappy marriages like her parents'—Rachel and Jimmy's twenty years ago when she was a little girl. Vi had said to Rachel—not to Vernon—only that "it wasn't meant to be." That was it. They had to accept the breakup without one question. We wondered what Vi would do when Rachel and Vernon went down. We meant got old. Vernon already looked ancient because of his rough face—the old scars from the fire, the one he had saved Rachel and Vi from, but not gone back into the fire to get Jimmy. Rachel was wearing more and more makeup and brighter and brighter colors, sure signs of old age. Vi's specialty was emergency medicine and skin grafts, and we had heard that she made her lowest grade on geriatric care. Nell and Richard Gilliam were there but looked like ghosts and we wished they hadn't come. We do that—go to parties to avoid being at home.

Sam brought photo albums not just from his Grand Canyon wedding— the helicopter, the bride standing in the wind, and the minister in sunglasses, and pictures of the limo that took them to the hotel with roses in the four-hundred-dollar-a-night honeymoon suite. We saw close-ups, of the roses and zoom shots of the fountains Sam and Teresa could see from their hotel room.

Sam had driven up for the reunion at River View with Teresa and his daughter, Tracy, from his first, long-term marriage. Tracy was just out of rehab for anorexia, Sam said in a disbelieving whisper. Tracy had brought with them her new fiancé and his children, so Sam had come with seven people, all packed nicely in the roomy white SUV, the one he had found on the internet out in Dallas. He was glad he kept saying to take rooms at the motel for the reunion, repeating that he knew our house was full. Only he could see that it wasn't. He could see that our daughters hadn't shown up. Jill told me on the phone that not coming would save her a bunch of money, and she hoped we could understand that she just couldn't make the reunion with all she had going on with planning the wedding, not that Bert was any help with it, which was going to be a big "church thingy."

I had learned, also on the phone, six months earlier, that I was going to be his mother-in-law. That's how Jill put it. She went on to say in that conversation that my voice sounded like "a blue-blooded/redneck-hillbilly." Defensively, I said that she knew that I had taught Latin, and she said that must explain it. I had laughed, again defensively, thinking she was being witty and that I had maybe missed a step, but I kept trying for her sake to say the right or almost right thing. I heard myself saying that I couldn't imagine what being an old Latin teacher had to do with the way I talked.

"You're killing me here." As if I were the murderer and she were bleeding to death. That had been our phone call.

Four months after the highfaluting wedding—she liked to use that phrase and leave off the final g, making fun, I guessed, of my accent—I am on the phone asking, "What went wrong?" I expected her to hang up on me, but I was also counting on her love of explaining how right she was.

"Bert, I hate to tell you, and I know you won't believe me, and I know that no one else will tell you, is deeply damaged. Or as I tell all my friends, a shithead. And I always add, it's no surprise. He's other things too. A liar, oversexed and stupid. I know you thought he was okay, would do for me. "

Like a fool, I had to ask her, "Then why did you marry him?" I heard over the line, a long sigh.

It had been a big deal of a wedding, as over the top as Sam's Grand Canyon thingy. The brass ensemble of the city's symphony had played in the church, all Broadway tunes, music I'd never heard at a wedding, but then that was my small potatoes view of the world. I don't think the congregation expected "Oklahoma" either because the minister looked toward the stained-glass skylight for help when he began the ceremony.

"I wanted to get married. Bert came along. I thought I wanted a big deal. I gave myself a big deal. I wanted to stick it to you and dad, make you pay through the teeth for all the shit you've given me. It was a big wedding or your divorce, and the wedding was a hell of a lot cheaper. I didn't think Bert would go so nuts. You'd have to know his family to understand the way they think."

I heard myself answer Jill in the sickening way I have developed since the wedding, seeming to acknowledge the truth of what she has said, and going on to another point based on the one she'd made, as if I accepted her premise, agreed with her and was trying to offer something new for her to demolish.

"But what happened that night when you locked Bert out of the house? Wasn't it just an accident that the dog got out and ran away? And anyway, didn't the dog come back that evening? Do you make your new husband leave because the dog got out, the dog who came home a little later, not hurt, not anything?"

"I knew you would be like this. Your phone is breaking up." Jill hung up.

So, with Jill and Bert's saving money for their doomed wedding, they did not come to the reunion, and when her sister heard that Jill wasn't showing up, she called, and said she was sorry, but she would have to miss it, and would I give her love to everyone.

Sam took note of our empty house, asked where our daughters were and then shrugged it off saying he and Teresa were comfortable in the motel. Tracy's boyfriend's kids loved the pool and the exercise machines there. Sam liked being able to get up and get free coffee at six in the mornings.

Sam is a part-time private investigator and told us about his cases, the last one took the cake he said. The murderer had taken a taxi to the people's house, killed the man first with a knife, then the woman, and put his bloody clothes in their washer, but then had forgotten to turn it on. Sam had been called in on the case because the murderer's family said that the wrong people had been killed and that Derwent had not meant to kill Tessa and Larry Uhl at all, but it'd been dark, the house was out in the country, and the murders were all a mistake. Sam had laughed and said he tried to explain that still, two people were dead, and that mistaken identity had nothing to do with the crime, and mistaken identity couldn't be used as a defense. Sam said he always knew what he was dealing with at crime scenes, and as I said, he kept looking at our quiet, empty house.

Then he launched into another story about a twenty-year-old case he'd been called in to work. He uses TV phrases like "perp" and "trace" but they fell out of his mouth in a natural way. This murder case had ended, at this point, at least, in a hung jury. The killer, he was sure he was the killer, had married the widow, been a father to the three young boys, but not a good dad to his own two sons who had grown up and hired Sam to get the case reopened. "Which I did," he laughed, adding that most murders are never solved, especially "the domestics." After the killing, the new couple, widow and killer, had joined the church, he'd quit drinking, and never laid a hand on his new children. His two abandoned biological sons said he used to throw them against walls, and once left them on the side of the road, put out of the car for being too loud.

"At least the case was all laid out on the table, and that satisfied me, to some degree anyway, and maybe the grown real sons. The adopteds, not that they had gone through all

131

the paperwork for being legally adopted, felt worse about it and stood by their killer stepdad throughout the trial, as did the church people who filled up the courtroom every day. Sometimes, it doesn't matter what happened in the past."

We knew that Irene would agree with Sam, and she would tell me—gleefully from her grave—that she was right again about what mattered and that she had not needed to come to the reunion anyway.

The Dodge and the Pontiac

We are flat on our stomachs, the three of us, a sister and brother and cousin, on the warm floor, listening to what's going on in the room below us. Mama is being yelled at by her brother, Talmadge, who is damning her to hell. It is much worse than what we are used to from daddy. Talmadge is accusing her in strings of curses. "You never have told the truth in your life, but you are not going to tell lies about me, and if you do, they will be the last words you ever get to say. You better button your damn lip. It's a dirty trick to play on me and Judy." It is sickening and thrilling to hear mama threatened by a man who had shot Germans and Japanese. He doesn't attack our Aunt Willow, mama's sister, who is down there too, sitting beyond our range through the heat register.

Daddy is sitting across the room from mama with his head down. Typical of him to be waiting for things to be over. We can see him when we lay our faces flat ears-down, next to the hot metal register over the wood stove directly below us, cutting our eyes at thirty degree angles and down into the anger and misery.

I was eight, my brother was six, and our cousin, eleven, from the more powerful family who owned a big farm and had tractors, but still used a team of horses to pull mowers and wagons. After working all day, Mr. Mitchell, the last man in the county who lived on their place to work the horses, let us ride them to the creek to drink and then back to the barn. He wouldn't drive the tractors, but our older cousins let us sit up high on the seats with them and steer.

Every now and then, mama is saying, "No, Talmadge, I did not tell anyone anything about you." We knew she was telling the truth. She never lied except about us—how sweet Eddie and I were and about daddy— "he is not drinking."

She does not raise her voice to her brother because he had come home, leaving their brother dead on Omaha Beach.

Celia pushes us aside to lay her face down almost on the hot grid to get a good angle on her mama who is sitting across from daddy and is as quiet, but for Aunt Willow, being quiet is unheard of and her silence is as frightening as Uncle Talmadge's threatening to kill mama for telling his new wife, Judy, our favorite relative—now married into us, "poor thing," mama always adds—lies about him. His life is no one's business. Especially a sister's. He knows that mama opened the letter addressed to him and read it, and then, she had told Judy what it said. He hopes that mama burns in hellfire.

We are scared rigid. Three petrified logs of children upstairs over the family fight. We'd be found someday and sent to a sawmill, and no one would ever know we had ever lived or ridden on tractors or horses named Beulah and Champ.

There is no way to get out of the house except to pass by the door to the dining room down the stairs with the huge jade plant on the landing, tiptoeing, we who have never tiptoed anywhere, don't know how, out into the darkness, to sit in the frozen 1950 Pontiac. Freeze outside or bake upstairs in the house—those are the two choices—only we needed to escape in order to freeze.

This was 1952 when Uncle Talmadge threatened to kill mama. Our green Pontiac by the back door was from happier times before we moved to the country near our cousins. To save the Pontiac, we used it only for emergencies. Daddy wanted us to drive the 1934 Dodge, the car he had somehow gotten to run. That night we had been thrilled when mama had said "Let's drive the Pontiac." We were primed for an emergency but not for murder. We were Methodist children. The seven miles up to our grandmother's house took no time in the Pontiac, and maybe we drove it that night because mama wanted to be in the Pontiac for our getaway, the car that would start on cold nights by itself, not parked like the Dodge on a little knoll to roll down, us pushing and flying alongside to jump in as it came to a little life.

Cremation Society

So, with all the funerals, we felt better after we joined the Cremation Society, the only club we were in. I didn't count the little country church as a club because Richard wouldn't go with me after a man had frozen to death less than a hundred yards from the church which was locked anyway. Richard asked what kind of club lets a man freeze outside its doors. He likes to try to make me see things his way. He grew up in the city so thinks he understands how limited the heart can be in a small town.

But it was a comfort knowing about the Society's twenty-four/seven service. I had seen with my own eyes two men in nice gray suits come for my aunt and take her out of the house with great care at three-thirty that morning last year, not bumping into the walls with the gurney, and going across the yard to their van, unmarked. Much better than the three-day ordeals we were used to when people died.

My Uncle Clement, for instance, who had served a brief term in the state prison in Richmond for mail fraud, had what was for us a state funeral, and gave my aunt—the one gently carried out of the house a year later—her best scenes of the heart-broken widow, her sons holding her up to walk into the church and to sit with her at the dinner that followed the long service. The minister had promised us all that we would be meeting Clement on the other side where all the rough places were smooth. The sons, Clemmie Jr and David, inspired by the injustice they felt had been visited on their father for simply using the U. S. Postal System, were both attorneys for white collar cases and had never lost in court.

We did not want such a funeral for ourselves. For one thing, our daughters were through with us and would never have shown up for such a "parade" they had said, knowing that I would like their use of Jane Austen's phrase even if I was a little sorry they did not want to come to my funeral or their dad's who was a much better dad than I was mom. Richard wants his ashes flying up from the car window as I drive on Route 6. That way he will escape at least some of the limits he lives with. He means speed limits, money limits, property lines, maybe marriage vows.

And, joining gave us a little taste of freedom. We could die anywhere, feel free to get sick, be in an accident, languish away feeling sorry for ourselves. Or, die from worrying about the miseries of our neighbors who although they went to my church, and "ran" it, Richard said, choosing the carpeting and roofing for the nursery school that never really caught on because it could not get the highest accreditation for the new kind of children that were growing up with ear phones and tablets. There were other reasons he never set foot in the church. These neighbors, the Larkins, did not get any of the benefits of being among the "churched," as a cousin calls us. Spiritual benefits, I mean. Other kinds, they got plenty of.

Linwood was certainly one of the unchurched. Richard would not admit that things might have gone better for Linwood if he had had some kind of group to belong to. Maureen, his nutcase sister did not count in anyone's book as a group of any good kind.

He had to be cut down from the tree— "up where the wind rocked" —by the rescue squad. We heard about it that night. He had tried many times with guns and pills, but this time with a rope, he'd done it.

In Florida, the time he had gone to live with some friends, he had come after them with an axe.

"But that was only once," Maureen said, adding that it was Linwood who had done the studding and sheetrock for the now-fifteen-year-old renovation of our grandmother's house, and done a great job. "Couldn't ask for better walls than Linwood gave us last summer."

It was a house no one in the family wanted, and we were beginning to think no one else did either because it had been on the market for five years, the price going down every year.

Two older men were living there rent free in exchange for their work, but Ray had been having problems with his blood pressure, and Jasper with his sugar levels, so the work had stopped. There were no doors hung and the stairs were only roughed in.

Linwood was known for his special skill with studs and sheetrock. He may have been close to fifty. Who would know except us that he had a Phi Beta key for his philosophy major, but that was when he was young.

He had been living in with his sister who hadn't had a job in years, so he was keeping her alive with his jobs hanging sheetrock, added to her disability check. I had read his thesis and hadn't understood a word of it, though I could tell that his sentences were shaped like parallelograms and three-dimensional rhomboids. Who cared that he could buzz saw geometric sentences from the air, ones no one except his teachers ever had understood, and they had forgotten him at the college that had given him a full ride to lift the GPA's of the graduating class, which he did. I was sure of all that being a teacher myself.

Brilliant students slip by teachers. By me, at least. It's the weak and slow who never leave you. Richard says it's the bad students that are the hope of the future. One older, or as we say, a "returning" student sent me his blog. He owns a restaurant now at the beach. Last year, my worst student asked me to feel his hair. I think he wanted me to know that he was not a black person with a black person's hair but a Puerto Rican with silky curls. That's what he said when I told him it wasn't appropriate for a teacher to feel hair, not of a grown man. He never handed in work on time and when he did, it should have gotten F's, but I gave C-'s.

Richard and I are not as happy as we like to think we are. It's all Richard's fault. The December weekend was a time I thought Richard and I were heading down to Charleston just to do something different though we had been there a number of times. We like that expression "something different." It's what Richard's dad always said about the same old things, and he meant it. Let me hasten to say that everyone in this story, speaker included, is over seventy.

Richard came home. Of course, he did, but I did not know that he would. I thought he was gone, gone—the way Linwood was gone, dead. Richard had just left after I had gone to school—a Friday. His note said, "Merry Christmas, Nell."

I knew that the note marked how far he had slipped into insanity. It had knives in it. A killer note. Did he think as he wrote it that he was ending our long marriage politely? Was he that far gone? Maybe he thought that the irony of the note would appeal to me.

A Big Deal

We buried daddy in the brown leather slippers he'd gotten at Christmas. No socks. There's nothing unusual in that. I know some people who've buried their loved ones barefooted and some who've shod their dead in their best. We chose slippers, a happy in-between. It paid off right away, for the night of the funeral, in my dreams, daddy got up from his walnut coffin and leaned conversationally against it smoking a Chesterfield Regular with no rancor about its being Chesterfields that had helped put him in slippers and walnut.

This lack of rancor was owing to death. Living, daddy was scorched with irritation and at the same time, softened by vodka. Vodka and cigarettes funeralized him as our local newspaper sums up last things. He stood there so warmly, so soberly, another blessing of the afterlife, and told me in a fatherly way which he had never had when he was alive, that I shouldn't make such a production of helping Austa—that's Mama—that it upset her for me to be so studiedly dutiful. His words were, "Sharon, don't make such a big deal of helping Austa." He never made any deal at all of helping her. It was amazing what being dead for three days had done for Daddy, though I preferred him alive. I know I did take mama's arm too carefully or bend over her too solicitously at supper when we had company.

Then I woke up, the kindly impressions lingering of daddy, the details of his crossed ankles, bent knees and

141

drooped wrists with the Chesterfield in his yellow fingers more vivid than the details of the funeral home where he lay waiting for us all to come and sit with him for twenty minutes talking about the size of the cantaloupes and the black-eyed peas coming in. Daddy's garden was known for its grocery store quality. "Looks store size and color," was a compliment.

His advice not to make a big deal with mama was harder to keep alive and vivid than that warm impression of him. It was such a mild revenge for becoming mama's nurse-companion to dramatize my goodness. My sighs emphasized my goodness. My groans accompanied the contortions necessary to get her inside a car; they follow my wheeze from stooping to tie her shoe.

A piece of Urdu comes to mind; unfortunately, it supports daddy's side of the argument, "A good deed recalled is erased," or something like that. I suppose the Urds (?) would agree with my paraphrase, "Obvious help is no help." This is not exactly true even if it sounds like grace itself—to help secretly. For instance, when there's a Volkswagen door and a prematurely ancient woman who is in pain and who must be helped through that aperture, any help—huffing and puffing—is good. St. Paul claims that God loves a cheerful giver, but a sullen one gets the job done too.

Like other families, we have dead members to deal with who haven't completely died. Still arounds, I call them. Aunt Tatie died five years ago. She had been to Italy four times and when she came home from the first two-week tour with her Mediterranean Society, she laid a brick patio herself and served us all espresso on it. She was seventy-five then. You don't expect a person like Tatie to leave the patio she had gone to such pains to build, sinking the bricks in creek bed sand, arranging them in fishtails and then having us all come, tactfully divided into political groups of cousins, for conversations, espresso and Italian ices.

The espresso reminded us stay-at-homes of motor oil, thinner only in its sharp, black aroma. Tatie's help to us was obvious, was studied, was even missionary. She called us her Calibans.

Her work was cut out for her. We read *The Thornbirds,* she was reading Manzoni and said if it was the pastoral we were after, we should look into *Adam Bede.* We said *The Far Pavilions* was what we were into. She was too solid to look stricken, but she came close.

Tatie had taught Latin for thirty years at the high school we'd all gone to, but my generation had elected Spanish rather than get trapped in her Latin class where we knew from her what she expected of her students. She wanted tears for Dido on her bier, she wanted kids to bleat in sing-song the pitched dactyls of Virgil.

Forget it, we said to each other and went into Mason's Spanish class where the hardest assignment was to make a papier-mâché goat and fill it with Christmas junk. Bill, my first husband, had taken Latin, five years of it, which is one reason she didn't criticize the marriage. And Tatie was one reason he wanted to marry me. Her and her patio and Virgil in the evenings.

I learned to be obvious, to make big deals, from Tatie who took care of Lou-Lou, her mother, for eleven years in a very splashy way. Talk about big deals. Talk about not hiding your light under a bushel. Tatie would call me and tell me how many times she had gotten up "in the night" to help Lou-Lou; she did get up and fix her hot oatmeal at three many mornings, I know. But she never did without almost instant replay on the telephone of the ordeal next morning to mama or me. Lou-Lou lived to be 103 when she got an engraved card from Jimmy Carter which she tore up because she had heard you were supposed to start getting them at 100 and she was mad that she'd been mixed up in a computer.

When Lou-Lou had to go to the nursing home, all of us cried, except for one, Tatie, who lived only a year alone. She buried Lou-Lou two months after she went to The Hermitage. Tatie's husband Walter had died in 1957. The patio was a great comfort that last year, she said, reminding her of Rome, of Florence, of what "could be."

She often explained to us the good and bads of "what could be" in great detail. We could get old. It would begin she said with our fillings shrinking in winter and rattling in their cavities so that when we ran or even walked fast, we would hear a little series of clicks, like little knitting needles. It was, she said, the sound of fate, snipping in the cavities of our sugar-crusted molars. These speeches were delivered superciliously, a word she taught us, but out of a teenaged deference to her, we never used to make her look good. We could nod and understand her when she used it. That way, whenever she said it, she was graciously including us nieces in her "It Pays to Increase Your Word Power" manners. It's hard to explain. What she meant was we should brush our teeth. This was the bad side of what could be. The good side was, of course, Florence, Dido, patios, and little cups of oily café. I cherished breeziness; I would say my friend Mary-Doug had "a touch of bulimia" and boasted of reading Ann Landers while vomiting. Tatie tried to correct me by saying, of course, girls had vomited in her day, not to mention Rome's, but they had had better sense than to mention it, much less brag about it. Celia was the cousin in charge of goodness. The whole pack of us wanted our goodness recognized underneath the dirty windshield of our personalities. I was known for my mealy mouth, but thought and think, I have a remarkable and unsung streak of honesty. No one has ever complimented me on this streak. Not Natalia who came home with me from college every weekend and knew our patio life.

My husband, this one, Lewis, loved me because I can adjust the rabbit ears so well that I can bring in channels no one else can without a roof aerial. He said it was symbolic of our love. He wasn't surprised to hear about daddy talking to me in a believable way. He said if I could pull in Baltimore across the Piedmont, and I hoped he meant if I could stay married to him, I could talk to my own daddy from the afterlife. He thought the advice was a little too good to be true, given that Big Austa—that's what he called mama—needed all the help she could get and she wasn't about to get any more from him at that point.

Lewis never got over the last time he took her to the store. She thought Mr. Stout had taken her Minute Maid juice, substituted Richfood, and charged her the Minute Maid price, $1.39 a can. Mr. Stout owns the grocery store and has better things to do than switch orange juice brands on his customers. Lewis had stood around trying not to get

145

upset. He said he finally had to go sit in the car and wait. When mama realized that she was arguing with Mr. Stout all by her lonesome, she came on out and got in, all by herself, because Lewis didn't offer to help her. Mr. Stout didn't either—for the first time.

This was the way we were living when Lewis left again. A far cry from his great Aunt Tatie's patio and trips to Italy and a Lou-Lou who could do the opening hundred lines of "Hiawatha" when Tatie called on her. They both had lived long enough, they would explain, to have grown up loving Longfellow; later they said they enjoyed his quaintness. Lou-Lou fell in with Tatie on things literary, as we all did. Her one objection to Tatie's taste was Walter, "the husband of the piece."

She even went along with the first husband, I mean, because he had tried to overcome his background of getting and spending by studying Latin. She was a "still around" by the time Lewis had made his entrances and exits as "the husband of the piece. So he didn't know Lou-Lou in the flesh; he had hardly known daddy, but he said he felt like he had lived with all of us from soup to nuts, to Lou-Lou and Tatie, to old Irvie, daddy. And, of course, he had The Brothers as he called them to fill him in on The Truth. The ghosts kept piling up. All the peculiar quietnesses came, I think, from all the "still arounds." Lou-Lou dismissed Walter with "inadequate." Tatie said Lou-Lou didn't have the imagination to fathom Walter's being.

"I guess not," we often heard Lou-Lou say to herself in the middle of one of her jobs. At that point, Tatie was putting Lou-Lou on a regimen, but to Lou-Lou the piddling little jobs seemed suburban, her word for silly.

Lou-Lou had grown up when the boys were dragging home from Appomattox, she had plowed with a mule, had lost a "blue baby" and a son on D-Day. We summed her up this way, "That Lou-Lou's been around." We taught her to say back, "For Real," or "For Sure."

Tatie and Lou-Lou competed to see who was the more observant, who could take in more of the life that was offered. The patio was a sort of stage where they sat in the evening and played one up in sensibility. Mama, Tatie's youngest niece, didn't fit into their owl and nightingale competitions. Mama was so modest, before her arteries got as hard as old leather shoe laces, that she would never put her return address on a letter for fear she'd seem to be demanding a reply. Daddy was so modest, he couldn't stand to be sober too often for fear he'd be too smart for us. He could understand mama, but that didn't make him like her any better. "You don't get married because you like someone," he explained to me.

Now I know what he means. You marry someone who's willing to admire something about you, like bringing in faraway stations. Walter may have been inadequate, but he was willing to admire his Tatie who would lean on her grubbing hoe and quote from Book Four, "At the cave, the storm. Virgil," she would add for us. Walter went bankrupt several times, losing two farms his father had left him. I've inherited a mixture of this willingness to admire, and I'm limited in the line of imagination so my big deals with mama don't surprise me. I think of my larger than necessary

147

gestures as, for some reason, boxes of limes handed up on salty ropes to those sailors with rickets or of explanatory semaphores to the world about being left twice "by husbands of the piece."

The way Tatie used to talk kills me as I think about it. She would actually fling open the heavy front door and murmur, "You wore your taffeta!"

"Can you believe it!" I'd say, sounding even to me, mealy.

"Of course, I believe it. I can see it even in this light. Belief doesn't come in as I wish you would."

"You know what I mean."

"Why can't you say what you mean?"

"It's mean to say what you mean."

"Don't be clever."

"We sound like a sit-com."

"Say stichomythia."

"Say what?"

"I know what it means. You don't. You didn't take Latin. "Tatie said Ladten. "You're letting all the heat out."

Those elaborate and playful entrances are gone with Tatie. Now we come in with a "How's it going," and "Long time no see." Tatie's funeral was not worthy of the Carthaginian queen. The Styrofoam and plastic baskets for the arrangements had to be forgiven. She would not have, and that was one thing that made us glad she wasn't there.

Just like I was glad daddy wasn't there to hear the choir moan "Abide with Me" for him. He hated country church music. In religion he hated little deals like a choir of six women, all with big pale glasses and dangerous-looking sandals. I wish I had mentioned his funeral to him. That would have taken the heat off me and my exaggerations with mama. I could have reminded him of Tatie's funeral; we'd had a good laugh at how un-Virgilian it was, how far from Carthage Tatie was resting.

We cousins sobbed, trying to atone for taking Spanish instead of Tatie's Latin. The Boston and Texas cousins said "super" and "no way" as they laid into the spread of cakes and ham biscuits. At Lou-Lou's funeral, Tatie had catalogued the decline in the funeral meats and been shocked that Mrs. Rollins had dared bring one of those box pudding cakes for Lou-Lou. "But Lou-Lou can't mind, now," my brother said as they put away wedges of it. In his fashion, he had loved Tatie and even failed Latin for her to prove it. "She would and she does," Tatie said, pinching the yellow damp leaves from her African violets that hung with purple velvet blooms.

At Tatie's service, I felt like all frivolity and chances for what could be had slipped into the ground with her. I'm sorry to say I realize now that by frivolity and chances, I meant my brush with Western Civ. Who will remark on my taffeta or regret my passing up Ladten so I'd know how to increase my word power? We had all let Tatie represent culture to us and had made fun of it and enjoyed ourselves as her Calibans as we went on happily to become personnel directors, administrative assistants, evaluators, and public relations and communications experts. We remembered

Dido as someone we had teased Tatie about. Rome was a place in Georgia or a place for lions and Christians, a Hollywood set.

Mama was a quaint person who said foreign lands and meadows instead of countries and fields. Tatie said Austa would like to call the Herefords, kine, and the mangy deer who ate the gardens, hart. Mama laughed when I reported this insult to her and said for the forty-eleventh time that she, not Tatie, had made the highest A in Cicero.

"But that was high school Cicero," she adjusted her retaliation's aim toward the truth, as usual.

Those times of arming the new generation in the old rivalries are over with Tatie dead, mama out in left field, and daddy a dead reborner, admonishing from across the bar, my tinkling cymbal. He must not know how far mama's gone back. I guess he can see my insides for the first time, but he is missing the daily news.

One Sunday when Lewis was at home he found mama peeling apples that weren't there in an undeliberate pantomime, slow and, well, senile. Lewis said his good side was brought out by his in-laws, dead and living: it's being hewn out of the bedrock of his indifference. He went and got three Granny Smith apples and put them in the yellow bowl. Then mama did better, but I, a true great niece of Tatie, and making what daddy would say was a big deal, took to my bed. I couldn't or didn't anyway, put real apples in the bowl. I preferred the complications of collapse to the simplicities of washing the three apples and plunking them in the lopsided bowl.

Later it came to me that trying to explain to daddy what living with mama was like now—she's free of his drinking and she's the one who's befuddled now—was as impossible as daddy's explaining to me from the aspect of eternity how I should act. He couldn't understand that mama is losing her footing as a separate person and is being absorbed, before she dies, into me. She's becoming a memory before her time, becoming a wraith as she stays a rock. It is easy for daddy, dead, to point out my big deals.

Left-Over Vistas

Making great efforts to bring news to people who already have the message drives them away from me—this took me the seventies, a long decade, to learn. Occasionally, I still tell people what they already know. Then I get nervous, seeing their faces go slack with "Well, what is she saying anyway." It's hard to stop, but I'm trying hard to shut up and let live.

Her name was Nell for Eleanor—we had been introduced just two hours earlier. As we slipped down the hill on the walk to the creek, she talked back over her shoulder to me, saying out of the corner of a fluted mouth, "I used to think Eleanor was the worst name and wished my mother had named me something ordinary."

I didn't feel I could tell her that Nell was the nickname for Eleanor and Daisy is for Margaret. For one thing, I was in a slow-motion run down the hill, braking in lunges, catching hold of little dogwood trees and twirling myself out of a straight shot at her bony shoulders. I outweighed her by thirty pounds and would have trampled her under the leaf meal as I told her what she should know—her own name. Spit flying as I twirled, I imagined gasping in her ear as I brought her down, her elbow stuck in the underbrush like an open safety pin anchor, "You are Nell. Like me. We are both Nells." But I kept quiet.

I want people to see my growth and development writ large. Every encounter, even phone calls, I try silence as a way of relating to people. It's pretty amazing.

Was she really Eleanor? All I knew was that she was the only woman at the party with mascara on. I wondered if she knew who Eleanor of Aquitaine was. Still, I wasn't going to tell her and have to watch her crinkled eyes and lips go smooth. She was tiny and fluted, and her personality rose out of her in nice little puffs. I was into my listening mode and made a promise I wouldn't talk no matter what I heard. This was a test: a normal-looking person who was called Nell and thought her mother should have named her a better name. In the old days, say twenty years back, I would have taken her on—her mother, family-naming habits, names and souls.

The other Nell's makeup was spread in thin pink and freckle-colored sheets over her face and when she smiled, it all pleated like a fan made of wax paper around her eyes and mouth. Over her eyes was a pale blue, so perfectly done that she shrieked laughing when the hostess, just home from an island, brown and smooth as a pancake in her linen shirt, told of the woman who "descended the river bank and brought back in one fist, a ring on each finger, fishing worms and fresh aqua stripes over each eye." We were all laughing, I thought, at the worms and rings, but Nell might have been thinking about how the worms were an excuse to sneak off and put on fresh eye shadow or how poorly it had been applied. But no, I wasn't going to ask.

We had finished lunch, the five couples and the hostess, when the walk was announced. Ten children, eleven adults all over thirty-five. Our girls, Lillie and Clara, were the wildest ones there. I never was introduced to one of the couples but learned their names from hearing their kids yell, Sunny, Bob, Bob, Sunny. Bob would finally answer. Sunny wouldn't.

153

Sunny finished off the wine I brought and told the table how she and her girls were heavy into canals. They took up subjects for bedtime stories, she said, implying worlds of motherhood that I with my two so-called children had only scanned like a Balboa. But unlike the iron hatted Spaniard amazed at the Pacific or the honey-haired Sunny, I had turned back toward the jungle and plotted out a survival plan. The father of my Lillie and Clara, Wendall, had not left us, but we knew he'd like to, which was almost as bad.

At first, I thought Sunny and Bob were doctors, from a story she told of their Emily crying out one night that a wasp had stung her. Sunny said, "Forget it, kid, you're going to sleep," and the next morning there was this wasp still wiggling in her sheets. You can imagine how down Bob and I felt about that.

I asked the hostess what Sunny and Bob did, and she said they were left over Vista people who had come to work in New Canton back in the sixties, bought an old house, and stayed.

Sunny invited all of us to come kill chickens with her later in the spring. She killed her own turkeys and chickens and talked about the advantages of letting the blood run out. She had a funnel and trough so the birds wouldn't flutter and flop spurting blood all over. She could tell home-killed meat from store-bought. I guess I thought she was a doctor from this too.

It was seventy degrees and February the nineteenth. I hadn't been out with a crowd of people for so long, I wasn't sure what to do. Maybe parties like this go on all the time, or maybe the crazy heat wave in February was messing with us.

Lunch was big platters of saffron rice with warm, barely frizzled oysters in the middle, scallions shooting out from under and the bread I'd made that morning. Then we all headed out with wine glasses or cups of coffee to go down the hill to the creek.

The hostess, Amelia Ives, lives in a slave quarter, the big house long gone. She has a trust fund, travels, and gives parties like this. Wendall had gotten us invited somehow and said I'd bring the bread and wine. I use my loaves of bread as tickets, but for the last year taking care of our children has cut us off of a lot of lists. Wendall says he's going to go by himself— "individualized social life" he calls leaving me and them at home. This party was the first thing we'd been to together in a year.

The plan was to walk along the creek for a ways, and then come back up behind the house. It's eighteenth-century, made with slave labor as my grandmother used to say and so nothing to be proud of nor preserve.

My grandmother tore down all the slave quarters on her place and wrote to the Society for the Preservation of Southern Antiquities that evil did not need efforts made in its behalf and certainly did not need commemorating. What would she say if she saw Wendall in his thousand-dollar Confederate uniform ready to reenact the battle of Sailor's Creek? He used to want me to dress up as a camp follower or a farm woman whose corn crib was going to be burned, but my grandmother kept looking at me from across the bar as she used to say she would, and I couldn't do it. That may

155

have been the beginning of our troubles, but there are so many beginnings, I think.

I had come to the party with a shopping bag full of bread and a vegetarian paté and wine. I was not that far gone that I didn't know that meat was out along with tobacco.

Wendall had so much wry affection for left-over Vistas, the vegetarians who had come from almost outer space to places like ours to help us. He made himself a hammer dulcimer to sing old authentic songs, but Lillie and Clara preferred Michael Jackson. At five and six, their minds seemed as set, but differently, as Wendall's. I cannot imagine choosing topics for bedtime, like canals. I wondered then how Wendall would adjust to Sunny's chicken processing. He hates people to jar his image of them, but that's exactly what I hoped for and needed to do with my new quietness. Besides, at that point I wasn't really sure what he saw in Sunny, but I could tell he liked it.

I was definitely surprised at Sunny and her killings. She said killing chickens when you were drunk and with friends was one thing, but killing one big turkey by yourself with no wine or stuff in the house was another. I noticed she ate very little of the paté.

In my newly established silence, I was doing a lot of work. Talking uses calories and when you stop, like smoking, you have all this energy left over. I had gotten up early to make James Beard's French style bread, which Amelia who had lived in Paris as much as in Virginia called baguettes. I don't think Sunny was sure what baguettes were; I wasn't, so I missed several compliments I felt welling up around the table with the forced forsythia in an old fruit jar in the middle. A simple "Nell made the bread" would have done.

While Sunny was twisting her long hair up on top of her head to let it fall while she went on about her new improved ways of killing chickens, her husband Bob was standing with the other Nell by the window that was thrown open. Amelia would never mar her house with storm windows and screens. It's preserved as was—I mean it looked that way. There was a phone, as well as water, and lights, but you didn't notice them. You got the feeling of being back a century. For a front door step, she had a big mill stone.

Bob, I heard, just had a book come out. Poems. All of a sudden, I was getting sick. The only other person I'd known who had a book come out was my ex. When I knew him, and *knew* was not a word I liked to use for him, he wrote poems.

Bob looked like a golden gorilla from behind as he stood at the window looking out, and Sue sat on the window ledge looking like a robin's broken eggshell, pale and crunchy.

I was hoping I could go on looking at them when Amelia said we couldn't waste the day and must go down to the creek.

Sunny led the way with a rope she picked up from the corner of the room, never bothering to notice the drama at the window. Sunny was a take-charge person and was down the hill and up a tree yelling "Come on, Guys," before we straggled out on the lawn, spreading out before the woods' edge, preferring the wild lawn to the straight drop Amelia was calling a hill. The kids were barking up the tree, thrilled with Sunny's Tarzan vision of things—the rope, a tree, a running creek. "Sunny, Sunny, get me up," they bayed. "Cool it, let Sunny get things straight," she said down to them from the limb she was tying the rope around. Richard was holding the ladder and having a blast, as we used to say.

The Poet, as I was calling Bob, and the other Nell were starting down the hill and I was right behind, in hotter pursuit than I intended. My husband was down at the tree with Sunny doing his sixties stuff, not coming on strong, but coming.

We're not left-over Vistas; we're Peace Corps returnees. I had not left my poet husband for the Peace Corps, but I wanted to. He had come out of the closet—poetically, I guessed. He was considerate, more than Wendall, who thinks I appreciate his healthier relationships.

That's not entirely true. Wendall stayed with Sunny the whole walk, and I was left with a choice of being with the kids who didn't want me ruining things or being with the other Nell and the Poet who probably didn't either, though they were still at the social stage of development where they needed a fifth wheel. This stage, I could have explained in detail had I been in my old explaining mode, but no, I was going to be quiet as the rope Wendall was wearing on his shoulder, left over from the swing. I would keep on bearing down on the new couple that had formed itself at the window, Poet Bob and the other Nell.

I am glad that the Bible and Jimmy Carter point out that adultery can happen right out in the open, in the eye. It was quite a happening going on just then, to use an old piece of slang. I hoped Amelia would rush down the hill from clearing away her grandmother's Havilland plates and be my partner. I would have welcomed some more stories from her trip to the islands.

Wendall was probably explaining how he made his dulcimer or sweated in his linsey-woolsey Confederate underwear, or how he dyed his sash with butternuts. I had ground up the nuts, but I balked at putting a pot of yellow water on the charcoal grill to stir the sash with a stick. I guessed that Sunny was going on about how she made her blood funnel. Each thought the other was interesting, and they were: Sunny and her home killings; Wendall and his left-over vistas. Sue was fascinating the Poet too, mourning her name, and he was feeling bad about his wasted gorilla good looks.

Children love adultery, at least the early stages when they are used as excuses to go on little outings, treats that involve a nice new person. I know I enjoyed going out with my father and Mrs. Knowles for ice creams and drives to Rock Castle. Lillie and Clara, though, might not have been up to such formalities, and I didn't know if I had the strength of character to insist that they stay home when Wendall offered to take them out of the house for the afternoon.

The last event of the walk but not of the party was the episode of the lost children. Naturally, Lillie and Clara were in the lost bunch. I knew that they weren't lost but had led an expedition deeper into the woods and were reenacting some galactic war. I also knew I couldn't look that casual and say, "They're not lost. They're playing." I knew Wendall knew too, but he asked Sunny to go with him down to the creek to look.

Back at Amelia's, we got into the cheap wine and felt February assert its real self. Amelia closed the windows and tried to start a fire but didn't have any dry kindling. I had started to bring some but had not wanted to look too obviously the know-it-all, the person who had always lived on the Rivanna River. We shivered and watched the only warm people in the room—the Poet and Nell my counterpart. They were talking about Masterpiece Theatre, whether the books were better, and then they went deeper with each other, asking where was the "Masterpiece" now in the Australian epics being rerun. Much quiet laughter. All the children were inside, doing lip syncs and gyrating in the basement rec room. Only two adults were missing, but vowed to silence, I partied into the evening.

White Women at Parties

Late in the year, we went to a lot of parties. The holidays sugared over terrible things, some new terrors for us. At those Christmas parties, we saw our first illegitimate white baby, a baby brought home in the regular old way, not hidden or adopted off or aborted.

There were, of course, the same old, regular terrible things at the parties. Unwanted aging women who had been used up nursing their dying mothers and husbands were automatically laughing softly, looking for new husbands to nurse.

Around here—this is central Virginia near the horse country, but not exactly it; the new South but not exactly new. We had the first black governor in the country and he had a wealthy white girlfriend—we still use girlfriend and date as if we were back in the fifties—who helicoptered to Richmond to see him—that's the new South. Their affair or dates or mutual use of each other ruined her and cost him his career—that's the same old South.

Black families had always taken in their children's love babies, but the white families went to Maryland for abortions. With the new fundamentalism everywhere, even on the campuses, abortion wasn't an option.

Kay's baby was beautiful with his presidential head, Roman nose, pianist hands, and Kay had that new mother beauty. He was named for his father, Marshall, and Kay's father, George. She called him George Marshall. No last name was mentioned. Kay was nineteen, a sophomore on scholarship at Sweet Briar, home for the holidays with the baby. She brought George Marshall to all our parties. I don't think she went to any young people's parties that year, just ours. We heard about the sessions with her lawyer. She was going to court in February to get support. The baby's father would have to support them. She had left school with a 3.5 average just before exams. Her major was geology. She thought she would live at home. She had five horses in her father's barn. Maybe she would take a few computer courses at the local college.

We all held the baby. She talked about George Marshall the same way we used to talk about ours. A little cereal at night, flexible schedules.

Kay was thin as a strap. It was Marie, her mother, who looked soft waisted as if she had just had a baby in late November. A tic ripped across her face with no warning quivers. Here it was, grotesque, then gone, a smile again. Several times I saw Marie's lips meet a glass and then stretch back in a flashing rictus. Bourbon dribbled down her chin and when Kay saw what her mother needed, she laughed and blotted her lips with her blue scarf. "You're drooling, Mama, like George Marshall."

The grandparents looked haggard, George and Marie, worn from farming and running the county extension office. Kay, the thin, new single mother, looked like a babysitter only she tossed the big baby and laughed too much, too attentive for a babysitter. She dabbed at Marie's chin expertly and stayed close by her as if she had two babies to watch.

George and Marie were giving this Christmas party at their lake cottage. The Canada geese had flown in that evening and filled up the three-hundred-acre lake. They called, stretched their necks parallel to the water and coasted down to light on the dark surface of the lake, all of a sudden floating shadows, not heavy birds.

We could see the black humps with the snake like heads flying low against the red sunset as we drove up to the house whose double-deck porches stared out across the lake.

We watched Marie. She held her shoulders back and walked like a movie star across the room even though the living room was tiny at the cottage. Still, her thin ankles flashed in glittering hose. Her water-colored dress whispered something sad. She was fifty-six and needed a rich husband instead of the one she had, George, who was land poor and with investments that ended up costing more than they brought in. The lake cottage was a good example. It was never rented out, so on holidays, Marie killed herself getting it ready for a party and we all went. The fire couldn't burn off the dampness or the mildew and we felt moldy, even though we knew Marie had been there scrubbing. George never said a word at this party.

Marie would have loved for Kay to have found a rich husband or even a poor one. Someone to help with the baby, with the horses, to get up at night. Marie wanted a husband to move in with them more than Kay did. Kay did not want to marry, ever. A baby's enough trouble, she said and then quoted Marie's mother, "A woman is always too young to marry." She almost laughed and said, "Look at you married people!"

Marie thought Kay's life was ruined with the baby. Kay thought she was just beginning to live with George Marshall. In his snuggler-sling, she went out feeding the horses, cleaning out the barn, and even gave him a ride with her. He loved it, she could tell.

Marie had told us that she asked the baby's father to the party, to spend Christmas with them and stay at the lake cottage. She said Kay had laughed and said it was a little late to start fixing her up. She only wanted to see him in court.

Kay wanted to talk to us, people who were forty years older than she was—Barbara and the new man, Harris Wilson, the new twosome. Kay sat next to Barbara very close and Barbara managed to treat Kay as if she were a patient. They couldn't get together on the ways they were treating each other.

Barbara did not mean to be insulting. She treated all of us if she were our nurse. We liked it and always felt feverish around her. She took care of her mother for years and talked to us as if we were flat on our back and not clear about whether we'd just eaten. We felt better at the end of each of her sentences. But she was not having the same effect on Kay who shone in her good health on the sagging sofa.

Barbara wore a crocheted lace collar that framed her face and a soft pastel sweater and slack set with a big jeweled belt. Her shoes were soft-soled slippers. We knew Barbara thought Kay was tragically ill. Case closed.

At last, Barbara struck the right note with Kay.

"Come for steaks so you can talk to my children and I won't have to. They quiz me to see if I am having any dates with Harris and I don't think it's any of their business, do you."

The children—a banker and an interior designer—came home once a year, not at Christmas. Barbara wanted to be able to say, "See, I have friends. Some people like me, even if you don't. They don't ask me about my dates as if I were a teenager."

Barbara's children wanted their mother to be married, out of their hair, but they did not want her to date anyone who might need nursing which was just the kind of person Barbara wanted to marry.

We knew the summer evenings out on Marie's dock, the snapping turtles floating with their heads just breaking the surface of the lake were something we'd gotten used to. But children frightened us. Our daughters were in college and sometimes we wondered if they liked us, but we never said anything like that. We were an upbeat crowd; our Lillie and Clara gave us advice about things our parents had never mentioned like menopause and adultery. Our girls knew too much about us. They had taken us to be dried out twice and had gone to family sessions.

"What can I get you," Marie asked under the ropes of running cedar she had plaited with sprigs of holly for the party. Her pearls with the diamond and sapphire clasp swung near our faces. She came back to us, a glass in each hand, bourbon and wine. She had a pine bough tied to the exposed beam of the ceiling. We had to stoop to walk under it. There was some real mistletoe tied at eye level too.

"Now, what else?" She laughed at us on her white speckled sofa.

Who said older women couldn't be sexy? If you'd been at those parties that winter, you'd know about leather pants, silk blouses, gold bracelets, shining hose, murmuring dresses—and not on Kay, the young, beautiful, lactating girl either.

A woman like Marie knew how to walk, how to lean over people especially ones with dead wives or who had had chemo themselves and appreciated swinging pearls and flashing ankles. Marie's sadness about her life was erotic. The men wore plaid vests and bow ties, hand tied. They voted against the black governor, but not because he was black.

"Look at me," she said, sitting down with us, pointing her foot and slipping her shoe, off and on, off and on. "I could have had it all. But here I am, like those stupid geese out there in the lake."

Marie did not want us at her party, but we were all she had. Who else would appreciate her movie star walk, her movie star daughter with movie star love baby? She wished she were anywhere else, but so did we. She did not want to invite Barbara and Harris Wilson who had not said a word at this party though they played bridge together and worked on the same committee, publicity, for the Historical Society. Marie did not want Barbara to compare Kay to her children who are single and live in condos and did not have babies.

As if she were the hostess instead of the unwanted guest, Barbara helped Kay with her long navy wool coat which came from a thrift store. We heard them laughing half to us, half to the bed full of coats. Barbara's voice rose, "When the fur coats were being handed out, I should have gotten a full length, not a jacket."

"No one offered me a fur coat," Kay laughed back, not bitterly.

Married men knew Barbara's story. They didn't understand Kay's story. How did the baby's father get away with it? George Marshall cried and grinned. The men were a little afraid of Kay. Suppose all us women had any baby we wanted. Barbara was the kind of woman they understood, and maybe they knew what made Marie the movie star type she was. Barbara knew her mixed effect—sadness, soft bosom, laughter, sympathy, bedside gestures, balanced drinks.

Sometimes, Marie ruined parties by apologizing too many times for the cottage, but at this party, she didn't. Maybe it was because George Marshall was there and had to be looked after, maybe it was because the baby's father might show up after all. What would he be called? Boyfriend, fiancé, date, friend?

Kay got up to leave, thanking Barbara for helping her again with her long blue coat. She had on white snakeskin boots, a pink denim mini dress, cut in a sculptured princess style, making seamed valentine frames for her breasts. She could flip down one side of the heart and nurse George Marshall under the big blue scarf, almost a shawl. Her hair was fly away in the ragged robin style, brown and soft. One arm held the nursing baby, one hand knotted up her hair so it stayed without pins or combs or rubber bands. We were amazed at everything about her. She had her mother's deep set blue eyes, only hers were outlined in smudged midnight blue shadow.

Marie brought the chafing dishes across the kitchen into the dining area. We gathered around and speared the last of the little sausages.

Harris Wilson acted like a movie star too. He looked like the alcoholic William Holden. When he left, he tilted his head to remove his hat so it wouldn't touch his wave. His blazer was double breasted, his overcoat was black cashmere and rode on his shoulders. He suited Marie more than Barbara. He had a drink in his hand. He was whispering into Barbara's hair. She drew away, saying "Of course, of course."

He turned in a slow spin, he said to us that he'd been drinking all afternoon, and left, not closing the door. With the door open, the wet Christmas air blew in. We heard the long calls of the geese.

What did he say to her we asked each other? Was it that he would call her tomorrow? We heard him start his Jaguar. We've seen it around and at Barbara's.

He was returning and paused at the open door. He stood there waiting for Barbara, not Marie, to walk him in. Like a nurse. We felt head colds starting.

Now, it was time for us all to leave. Harris Wilson turned to our nursing mother. "What's this, what's this! Madonna and child! How marvelous, a living crèche. When I was last in Florence, the Madonnas broke my heart."

"I was in Florence last summer as part of an internship. Not for restoration, just rocks. Stones not of Venice, but any

Italian stones are my line." Kay shifted George Marshall to her shoulder and patted him.

Barbara walked noiselessly across to the table, complimented Marie on the hot chafing dishes, and was saying she was glad she could come at the last minute. Marie was too and managed a drink without the tic making her lips go slack. She was watching Kay and offered to take the baby.

"I'm fine," Kay said, laughing up at the new husband for Barbara.

We had stories to tell about the closed landfills, the suicide of the dentist who stepped out of his office on Route 5 into the path of the semi, the calves trapped in the sudden ice on the ponds last week. We had children to describe and brag about. In this way we were superstitious: saying good things about our children—grades, teams, trips—these would protect them and make them love us more. We came close to lying when we felt for the high reaches of bragging with our fingers. We wanted our daughters to mop our chin as Kay was ready to do again now for Marie, but we didn't want babies to come home with Lillie and Clara from college. We were white people and knew we were inadequate. We would pray to be forgiven, in whispers, to the extent that we understood our lives at midnight service on Christmas Eve, Lessons and Carols.

Harris Wilson took a new glass from Marie and watched the swing of her pearls. He felt at home in this room of problems. We had heard how his wife lasted as a vegetable for ten years. He had round-the-clock help and no one blamed him for going out, dating before the funeral. We bet that Barbara and he would be married by next Christmas.

George Marshall finished nursing, his head lolled back sleepy, happy. His grandmother was laughing between the lightning flashes on her face.

Sabastian

Valerie had asked for it—the humiliation—the coals that burn for years to punish us for loving the wrong people.

Hal did not love her. Period. He tried to, and his effort humiliated Valerie more. She had been ready to jump out of a window or plane, swim an ocean, and convert to an Eastern religion for him. HAS IT BAD had been written all over Valerie, and so Natalia, her best friend and also Hal's cousin, took it on herself to tell Hal what he must have known or should have—that Valerie loved him, and then Natalia arranged a weekend for the three of them at Hal's in Raleigh. The plan was that Hal would give in, love Valerie back, and propose marriage or a life together of some intense, desperate kind. Knowing what was what, Hal would then act. Knowing how much Valerie loved him, he would respond in kind. This was the theory, and evidently, Hal promised Natalia that it would happen. He would speak, as they said in old novels. But he did not. When Valerie learned about what had been planned for the weekend, she felt worse than ever. Obviously, Natalia lived on a different planet to think that she could plan people's lives. Her plan was a secret until it failed. Valerie had had no idea, was completely in the dark.

This happened during the last days of Gulf War in the early nineties. Valerie had just gotten a current events project for her Special Ed students up on the bulletin board about oil wells and Muslims when suddenly the war ended or seemed to end. She made a burning well out of gold foil for her students, and gave it to Tom Dacre, whose father was mobilized and sent to Kuwait, but was back at home in three months, selling insurance. He brought each child in the class a zip-lock bag of sand.

Just before this trip, Valerie had killed a cat named Sabastian, one she had gotten from the animal shelter as a gift for Hal. Later, Valerie tried to press Hal's non-proposal down into herself, so far down, that the evening in Raleigh when Hal could not bring himself to love her, was buried beneath the cat's death and all mixed up with the Gulf War—out of chronological order. Two years later, she can feel flames deep down in her tamped down under one of the organs her driver's license donates to science in the event of her death. Her throat stays inflamed and she has a recurring feverish, dry cough. Two years is too long to have a cough.

Natalia's medieval efforts on Valerie's behalf to arrange this marriage nearly killed Valerie, though she can appreciate, in theory, the planning and the secret thrills Natalia and even Hal must have felt for some months before the October visit as they discussed long-distance how great their lives would all be. Marriages should be arranged.

Deliberately Valerie thinks of the dead cat Sabastian and the burning oil wells in Iraq instead of the night in Raleigh. She has never asked Natalia to explain what happened with Hal. After all, Valerie was there and saw it all, lived it all.

"I think so, third weekend in October? Right. Got it. Perfect. Cool. We'll be there." This was the part Valerie heard, innocence itself—the plan for another one of their trips to Raleigh.

Valerie was Hal's friend who had brought him so many gifts, who made him laugh, who listened to his earthworks sculpture plans, who had backpacked through Wales with him. He did love her. Right?

Valerie knows that she should feel that this non-event, something that did not happen is not as terrible as what actually did happen—to the Kuwaitis, for example, who, she has read, had been discoing when the Iraqis invaded. The non-event should not feel as terrible as killing the beautiful cat. But it does.

Natalia and Valerie, friends during and since college, both have wanted Hal to marry Valerie from the moment Natalia introduced Valerie to Hal. They are embarrassed to be hung up on getting married, but with each other, they do not have to apologize for feeling old-fashioned and wanting proposals and marriages, then babies, and then divorces if necessary.

Valerie's mother could see immediately that Hal did not love her daughter; she could see that he is in love with another person. Himself. She does not say this to Valerie because she loves Valerie, and anyway, there is nothing that she could have said that would have stopped the plan for another weekend in Raleigh, even if she had known that this one was The Weekend. Natalia herself loves Hal and has since they were nine when their families lived with each other for a year when her father lost his job, but she will find someone else to marry which she can because she is beautiful all the time while Valerie is beautiful only when she feels loved. There is love on all three sides of the triangle—Valerie, Natalia and Hal, best of friends. Plenty of it to go around, so why not direct the flow a little.

Still, they should have known. When Valerie looks back on the weekend in Raleigh, she makes the death of the cat replace the unrequited love story, or tries to. Guilt is easier to live with than humiliation, which is so personal in its heat-seeking accuracy, so private in its torments. Goes for the eyes and mouth.

Sabastian, the name on his file, was a Chablis-colored Siamese. Two weeks before the trip to Raleigh, Valerie had gotten him just before he went into the decompression chamber at the animal shelter. She wanted to take a Siamese to Hal. The shots and spaying cost a hundred and forty dollars. Sabastian had been intended as a gift for Hal who would appreciate his regal beauty, one of the many gifts of this caliber Hal has received from Valerie. These gifts are the basis for her love for him. She gives gifts and Hal accepts them with deep appreciation of her understanding of his need for the quintessential whatness of things. He gives nothing back except his full attention to the gifts, and that is one of his appeals—self-sufficiency. Hal is appealing to all women except Valerie's mother.

For three years now, Valerie and Natalia have driven down to Raleigh from Richmond with the car loaded with gifts for Hal. But the Monday before the trip, Valerie killed Sabastian with an application of NO-TICKS NO-FLEAS. He had licked the NO-TICKS off, drooled two fangs of foam and died, shocked, Valerie felt, that after two weeks of Norwegian kippers, Moist Bits and television on a pillow, he had been splashed with a milky fire, which his long tongue sent back to his shoulders, couldn't wash away. Sabastian had died a terrible death, not the one that would have been his at the animal shelter if no one had rescued him, an unlikely fate because of his beauty and pedigree, though maybe these were intimidating to people looking for a cat to take home to the suburbs. There were three pages of his lineage. Another person would have taken him home to a long, safe life. Any other person would have been better for Sabastian than Valerie.

Sabastian. He loved to walk across furniture and quietly jump in high arcs across spaces. He startled Valerie with his gravelly purrs and demands for affection. "Pet me, foolish woman," he said over and over, small pebbles like pearls rolling around in his throat.

In Valerie's classroom, there are no misdiagnosed students—they all really belong in class for the educable, mentally retarded, the EMR's. She had hoped with each one of the parents that maybe the paperwork was wrong and there had been mistakes in diagnosing the trouble, that, in fact, the children were geniuses, just maladjusted or weird, nerds, doofuses, anything but real EMR's, maybe even idiot savants, not just retards, rejects, as the other kids called them sometimes in the halls.

Valerie knows something of forced labor—her own and her pupils'. Herding her students through the specially designed classroom and bright packages of learning activities has toughened her, but the puzzlement she sees come and settle on her students' faces is sanctioned by the state. She has a three-year provisional certificate in special education

175

only because the principal couldn't find a qualified teacher and pushed her application through.

After watching Sabastian die from her ministrations, she thought that she understood how a reluctant, ordinary German soldier must have felt, dealing out torture to the innocent. She is horrified at what simply following directions—pulling levers or turning nozzles—can do to skin and fur.

The bottle of NO-TICKS NO-FLEAS did not say for dogs only. Valerie's psoriasis came back, mocking her guilt for Sabastian's writhing with its mild pink, puffed splotches. Her elbows and knuckles dried and lifted off in flakes. She looked and felt older than twenty-three. "Isn't the man supposed. . ." her mother has asked Valerie over the phone about all the gifts loaded into the car for Raleigh. Valerie's mom hopes to stop the gifts with the question, but she knows that her daughter goes on making Christmases for the young man with a shaved head and earring.

"Let me send Hal presents. Val! Wasn't it Emerson who said the only gifts should be flowers and books?" Sometimes she adds, as if Valerie's father were dead and mourned, "What would your father have thought," instead of happily divorced and remarried.

"Emerson didn't know as much as he thought he did," Valerie says bravely into the long distance to her mother. "You just have this thing about Hal, but thanks for all the food you sent last week."

Valerie fills the car with slate from an abandoned house's roof, copper pipes from the dump, and relishes, both chow-chow and chutney, canned peaches and tomatoes she has made following her grandmother's recipes. She has just tried cold packing produce in mason jars. When the car is full, she and Natalia set off for Raleigh where Hal has his small colony of admirers. Then, the empty car, a Nova, comes back to be filled up again. It takes about a month to load up again. She has read that cooking is a sign of sexual repression and avoids that painful truth by saying as she makes focaccia to take to Raleigh that she knows all about that stupid repressed-slash-sex stuff. Hal is delighted with her gifts, heats up the bread, and tears into it with his teeth that have never been drilled, and says the presents show that no one knows him, his soul, the way Valerie does. His gratitude and appreciation are what have confused Natalia and also Hal, so much that they both think that he is in love with Valerie and all that is needed is a moment, a weekend, for the long hoped for declaration or proposal to come.

Valerie says to herself that she may know his soul, but not his other parts. Natalia knows something of how Valerie feels, loving Hal as she herself does. Hal does love the loads of gifts. It is simple, the solution: Natalia's friend and her cousin should marry. Why not? Natalia wants them to get married and then she will find someone—no problem—and they will all get on with the next part of life. It will be easy. Their babies—Valerie and Hal's will be adopted because of the world population explosion—will grow up together, start businesses or go to graduate school together. Something.

This trip is the trip to end all trips and to end the extension of their college life into real life. It's time for another life. They are finding out that it takes a lot of planning to have babies in modern America or to have sex with the person one wants to have it with. It's not a natural event in the lives of young women, not as simple as it seems now that everyone knows everything about sex in the post-revolution.

Natalia and Valerie feel this modern difficulty, and they envy in one way being a woman in the Third World or even in Europe where pregnancy is easier to achieve: a young woman is taken advantage of or married straight from her father's house. They know that the girl bride's father may be at home beating her up, but at least he is not divorced and remarried, and is at home. Valerie and Natalia know they are stupid and reactionary, maybe immoral, to feel this way. They know that women are burned alive in India who have dowries that are too small.

But, each young woman wants a baby. Period. They need husbands. They have had courses in gender constructs and images of women in literature, but they know when all is said and done, women still have to get married.

"It was different, gardening and canning for seven children, Precious." Valerie's mother tried to stanch the flow of gifts to Raleigh by invoking family history about canning and slaughtering stock for food for the winter. When she visits Valerie and Natalia in their Richmond apartment, she sees the car half-filled with gifts parked at the curb. She knows they drive Natalia's car to work and save the Nova for packing up for Hal in Raleigh.

"It's not like that now. Survival is not where it's happening, Mama," Valerie explains, satisfying neither her mother nor herself. She added, "This is art-canning. I doubt if these Mariglos will ever be eaten; these tomatoes are to look at." She knows how foolish and desperate she sounds to her mother.

The Nova gassed up, ready to leave for Hal's, Valerie looks through the locked car window at the car keys sprawled on the floor by the gas pedal. She is not worried because, anticipating something dumb like locking up the keys, she had left a crack in the window for fishing a coat hanger through. The suitcase and duffel bag are already in the trunk with more slate, and the country ham she has baked is wrapped in tin foil in the cooler in the back seat.

"Wouldn't you like to go out to a nice restaurant, sometimes," Valerie's mother has asked, heartbroken about this daughter who takes food, slate, copper pipes and now a cat to a man. She had tried to dissuade Valerie from the Siamese. "They are crazy, one, and two, maybe you give Hal too many presents," she said, generalizing her daughter's blandishments, shameless, to someone who looks like a convict.

"Conventions are not all bad," she tells Valerie, generalizing again, this time to take the sting out, making a blunted attack on the situation. She tries to imply that while every woman knows that a man needs a wife, a woman needs many other things besides a husband. But these generalities do sting when Valerie applies them like poultices to herself and her situation, if it is that, with Hal. She sometimes worries that she is caught in a self-fulfilling thing recently diagrammed in a workshop intended to update her skills with her EMR students. If a teacher sees the students as hopeless, they will be. Students sense their teacher's vision of them and give up hope <u>or</u> take heart; when they fail it's because the teacher expects them to.

So Valerie tries in her life to break the self-fulfilling contract, not just with her students. She leaves cracks in car windows to second-guess herself, to beat the prophecy out, to run faster than its time bomb, tick-ticking. She tosses the ball up slowly in a big underhanded swoop like her students learning to play a semblance of softball, then she runs, cartoon fashion, faster than the ball is falling and stands waiting to catch it so it won't bounce away disastrously. In the Hal thing, she does not know what to do. The ball is up, over their heads. She is running to catch it, she sees it black against the sun; yes, the ball is high, a dot, and headed down.

De-ticking Sabastian was to make him a trouble-free gift, like herself, for Hal. She agrees with Natalia that she would be perfect for Hal with her outdated skills and virtues—she is no trouble, she the 1990's version of an old-fashioned wifely person who preserves food to save lives in the winter. From two window boxes, she can grow all the ingredients for long pans of ratatouille and bowls of gazpacho. Last year she made Hal an Irish fisherman's sweater, even treating it with lanolin to waterproof it authentically. She has a job that she wants to keep in spite of its many cruelties to children (where else would they go if not to her classroom?) her whole life, with time off for having her own babies. She is a workaholic who is happy being one—maybe that's what the word means—anyway, she deals with it.

However, her perfect fit for Hall has never been discussed; there is no need to between friends. All is clear and assumed except that Valerie does not know that the proposal of marriage is planned for the late October trip to Raleigh. Raleigh's swampy lakes are a far cry from the Irish Sea's frozen crumpled cellophane where Hal will wear the sweater. Hal wants to have a studio on the coast of Ireland, she knows, after Raleigh, as she runs ahead to catch the thought that has occurred before—that she is a fool. Worse, she is silly. She knows it, as she keeps on knitting—figuratively speaking, since the sweater is finished. She's running to catch her slow high ball. Tossing and catching her thoughts. She will not fulfill the prophecy, but change it through dint of mental effort and a good heart, not to mention the sex which must follow as they are modern, healthy Americans, and which she is sure from observation and reading, is a powerful ingredient to be added to the friendship with Hal. He will, she hopes, need her in a sexual way. She already needs him and has since she first saw him. Sex can be a practical thing like canning.

When she misses the ball after running to catch it, she feels sick.

The NO-TICKS NO-FLEAS had worked on her mother's long-haired cat, Custard, so Valerie predicted, confident that she was arming Sabastian against the dry weather ticks in Raleigh, that she was taking care of some part of the cat's future with Hal. Treated, the beautiful cat could loll in the yard while Hal welded and riveted his junk sculpture. Sabastian would leap from cantilevered hunks to extended axles pronging out toward nothing. She had envied the cat's future there in the glare of the sun and whoosh of the blowtorch, making blue and green flashes in Raleigh nights.

181

Custard never bothered to lick himself when Valerie had rubbed him down with the solution. He was not fastidious like those crazy breeds, her mother said, and finally with some exasperation at Valerie's suffering over a cat who was condemned to die at the animal shelter anyway before he had his reprieve, she resorted to the specific and the obvious: Valerie had not meant to kill Sabastian. As if intention and pain were clearly connected.

When Natalia hears the story, she says it was an accident and that the cat was or would have been, the perfect cat for Hal. The one word Valerie's students can call out perfectly is "accident" when the tempera paints spill or they collide with desks. Yelling the word helps their bruises and cuts which happen every day in spite of Valerie's preplanning and second guessing their lunges and bolts, their toppling and stampeding into a corner. She hopes Sabastian yowled out "accident" before he squeezed up under the air conditioning unit where she found him swollen and grinning.

On the road to Raleigh, Natalia will enjoy the story of the keys fished up through the window and why the window had been left open. Natalia changes Valerie's view of the death of Sabastian. Sure that a Siamese cat was the right thing for Hal, after the accident, Valerie now claims that she had not been sure. Valerie repeats what her mother had said about Siamese being so crazy they didn't live long anyway.

Natalia agrees because she loves Valerie and wants to help her tell the right story about what Valerie had done. Valerie sees that Natalia loves her and is trying to help her change the way she looks at this murdered gift to Hal. Natalia is the best of friends, according to this standard of love, but Valerie's mother thinks Natalia is pulling Valerie toward disaster. Hal.

And so, the young women are driving to Raleigh from Richmond to spend the weekend with Hal. Valerie won't know what was planned for six months.

Hal is already an associate professor of landscape architecture and thinks that he can change the world by re-designing the contours of the earth. Or something like that. Valerie and Natalia aren't sure how minds and earth connect, but around Hal and his big sheets of blue prints for new cities, it makes sense. Houses will jut out of banked crescents to give prospect and community. It sounds fine even though Valerie thinks community is a dream, coming as she does from the rural county where there are many prospects but not much community. Hal grew up in the suburbs of Baltimore and she thinks some blighted nostalgia for the pastoral Great Depression his parents talk about has thrown him off track about community and prospect and the way people live together. He won't listen to her, seriously, about the real life in the country. Hal likes medieval-looking women and luckily the retro-sixties' style—long tendrils of hair, faraway eyes, embroidered clothes—is coming back, though mixed with rapster-punk. Natalia looks thirteenth century except for her platform slip-on shoes, but Valerie has looked like the 1950's since she was eleven. Natalia, who loves Valerie for her efforts of imagination, she calls them, tells her not to be so preoccupied with her fifties' hair and body. Valerie's hair, like all the women's in her family, is cut in the old poodle or bubble style in spite of mousse jobs to flatten and grease it down.

Valerie knows that Hal loves Natalia more than he does Valerie because Natalia looks and thinks like he does, and they have ancestral luck and symmetry in their long bones and deep eyes. Valerie, standing between them, is stumpy. Valerie doesn't mind substituting for Natalia if she can manage to squeeze herself between them; it's pleasant impersonating a beautiful woman. Love is physical, in the whole sense of the word, not just sexual, she thinks. Maybe life is entirely physical, as it is for her students. It's a distressing but obvious thought that recurs as they drive south on Route 95.

Instead of being jealous, Valerie grows taller and her cheekbones wing out around her eyes when she is with Natalia. They are perfect friends, because for one thing, of this physical difference. Natalia graciously envies Valerie her "personality" and dismisses the exhaustion it costs. She loved Valerie's dinner parties for all the stories Valerie tells as she cooks. One of her student's mother hides when there is company and the father must entertain the visitor, but the mother hides in the car in front of the house so the guests see her sitting there. Valerie tells the story with the same pauses and glances that the visitors must feel when they come to visit the family with the mother in the car. Natalia made Valerie tell Hal this story twice, repeated immediately, and they had to lie down from laughing so hard. It's not that funny to Valerie though she knows how it sounds and enjoys seeing her beloved Natalia and Hal stricken on the floor. She had imagined Sabastian wandering between them, bored and leaping away. Natalia wanted to get this marriage thing settled once and for all with Hal. Natalia is feeling new urgency—her birthday is coming, her putative baby needs a father, one she has not had time to meet, she has been so preoccupied with Valerie and Hal. Hal has finished a crowbar sculpture and wants them to see it before it is hung in the University's gym entrance. He wouldn't mind if it fell on some of the jocks, he wrote in his last letter to them both. Natalia has decided that Hal and Valerie must get married before Christmas. She has planned the proposal over the phone, and Hal has agreed to pop the old question. They must have laughed as they planned, all high hopes for the prospects and community embedded in the plan. Valerie and Natalia have announced to themselves and each other that they are ready for babies, which mean husbands. Neither one knows that she is stepping off the edge of the map. In fact, both feel the most ordinary of readiness, like six-year-olds feel a reading readiness, even EMR's.

Natalia who has had marriage proposals on first meetings, not to mention, dates, feels she cannot pick out a husband until she has Valerie settled with Hal. Natalia knows that his continental-sized ego makes him understand that he is necessary for any woman's existence and he is willing to lend himself to a marriage. He goes along with Natalia's plan for a couple of reasons. The coast of Ireland can be lonely, he is sure. He loves to hear Valerie's stories. There must be children who need teachers in Ireland, so a job won't be a problem for Valerie who can support them.

Natalia is beautiful; Valerie is not, but has this good personality striated with interesting violent crying spells. She wishes it were the last century so she could carry smelling salts with her to use when she felt a fit coming on. Her short hair would look even funnier then, Natalia laughs. She refuses to take Valerie's suffering over her crying and hair and hips seriously and says she has the classic Gibson girl body. But not the head, not the face, Valerie moans. No, she got Natalia's floating hair and no-hips, Natalia agrees, not impressed with how perfect she is in her vintage swirling skirts or black tights and little white tops. Natalia worries about real issues, she says, like her health—how her stomach, throat and head feel; her beauty makes her emotional life easy for her in a way that Hal's confidence in his talents makes his life easy, but strangely enough, on the downside, Natalia has no confidence in her health. She is always resting and taking vitamins or exercising and then resting, and then drinking a health drink. If anyone laughed at the crowbars, Hal would shake his hawk-set head sadly at the lack of perception of the powerful, he calls it. He wants to express this power that has been misunderstood all along. He gets smashed cars from a compactor and makes the sculptures, and it is true that he's getting known for his work which looks like larger versions of the stacks of things Valerie's students make all the time.

Natalia admits to her beauty without embarrassment. She told Valerie, who has always been fascinated by it, that she never looked in a mirror except as a reality check on her general health, that the greatest plus for beautiful people is that they don't have to try. She means socially. She is more relaxed in a group of strangers than with friends because there, her existence is enough. They look at her and let her alone while Valerie is killing herself thinking of the right questions to get people going on their lives or the right stories to tell. Valerie can get Hal talking about his plans quicker than anyone, his dark silences evaporating as she listens to him talk. It is Natalia who cannot call him out from his darkness. If she could, she would have married him herself in spite of being cousins.

Valerie's good humor is always masochistic so no one minds being around her. For example, her long funny stories about her family, how they keep adding smaller and smaller rooms to the house as failures keep moving back home to live. "To fight," she says. The small rooms were to keep down the number of fighters per room. She fears they will partition the huge kitchen so they can have one like Valerie's in the city.

"Night falls on the city," Hal introduces parts of the day as if they were his productions. He is lying on the black grass resting his head on one of his stacked sculptures called #12. He goes on. "And on," Valerie's mother would say if she were there to hear him on the power of art in the world. "The what in the where?" her mother would ask, not wanting an answer.

The ham and peaches chilled in the cooler had been delicious for supper. Now night falls in the sculpture garden, just as Hal said, the moon hitting on the soldering drops. Hal keeps saying the word "Finally," and Natalia goes into the house to bed. She must get her rest like the ancient crone she is inside her body. They all laugh at the beautiful Natalia and her health worries.

Finally, Hal has met someone, he is telling Valerie this secret that he has not told Natalia; in fact, it has just happened. "On Thursday," he is saying up into the dark air, "Just this week."

He is mesmerized by his words, "On Thursday," as if he were saying "Holy Thursday." Valerie starts running to catch the ball, the heavy athletic kind. It takes all her strength to catch it. She stumbles and her head comes down close to the ground as she runs along stretching out her arms, not dropping it.

"Her name is Claire. She paints."

"Is she the one who is coming over in the morning?" Valerie asks, stupidly reaching out for a convenient crowbar.

"Yes, she will love your ham and peaches, and your story about the small rooms in your mother's house. Maybe I can bring her up to Richmond to see you and Natalia. When I have time."

The night is still falling like the ball.

"Let me tell you about Sabastian. I almost brought him to you, but he met an unexpected fate." Valerie starts, and the kingly Hal settles into the angle of the metal base and looks warmly at her. He feels good that he has told her about Claire, and they can both tell Natalia about this new development in the morning.

Picking Up the Dead

Waiting for a sixteen-year-old girl who tosses her hair like a pony to come interview him about being old and sick is insult added to injury. Milton Parker is not old, he's fifty-one and dying.

Holly Ann Rodgers has a social problems project due next week. They've been studying aging, and she thinks she will get extra points for visiting a cancer victim. Besides, he lives right across the road from her family.

Last night Milton decided to burn down at least one of the Rodgers' chicken houses. The idea came to him as he looked at the moon as it floated by his window; it was not the high glider of his healthy years, but a low swinger that looked exactly like the bulb in his oven. It was surrounded and at times covered by lacy carbon flakes and bubbles. Milton was sorry to see the moon look as bad as he felt. The moon and clouds should be beautiful, but blaming himself for the way the skies looked made him feel sicker. The carbon flakes needed to be burned away from the moon so it could shine down the way it used to when he was well. That was how the idea of burning down one of the Rodgers' chicken houses came to him. From the moon. This is a sure sign that he is a dangerous man and it's a good thing his weakness slows him down. Otherwise, who knows, he might burn up the county.

The morning of the interview with Holly, as he fixes a breakfast he knows he cannot eat, the idea of burning down a chicken house gets clearer in his mind. He turns on the radio for the morning farm report. Ed Yancey's flat voice that he has listened to all his life sounds like a stranger's. Soybean and hog prices are up, but all Milton can think of is his fire, how to start it and how to get back home and in bed before anyone sees him. He'd be the last person anyone would suspect of setting a fire. Maybe if people knew what he thought about the Rodgers, he'd be arrested first and questioned later. His reputation and his cancer give him a fire wall to hide behind.

He boils grits, fries bacon, and even makes some fake red-eye gravy for the grits. The biscuits from a can look like wilted marshmallows and would taste like them too, if he took a bite. With his brewed coffee he is ready for Holly Ann Rodgers. The smell of bacon and coffee and the dirty dishes and pans give the house a false lived-in air which he appreciates, more than she will.

When Holly Ann starts off the interview trying to ask him about how it feels to have cancer, she doesn't want to say the word cancer. "You know what I mean, how does it feel, I mean how do you feel about yourself?" She writes her question down in her Garfield notebook.

"I'm mad at the world, if you want to know, and I don't care who knows it. Write that down and smoke it." He's too weak to hurt her feelings and she smiles as if he is telling her she is pretty. The fifteen minutes pass in a flash because Milton spends the whole time asking about her parents' chicken houses. It's okay with her because she knows a lot about poultry science and plans to go to Tech to get a degree in it. He asks her what's the worst part of raising a hundred thousand chickens and is pleased with her answer. "It's really not too bad after you get them started, except for picking up the dead."

Milton pours himself another cup of coffee as Holly Ann goes on to elaborate about the pluses and minuses of chicken farming. One of the minuses is that in a large chicken house a chicken farmer can expect a certain number of chickens to die every night. Holly Ann gets to pick them up every morning. The arrogant curl to her lip as she explains it to Milton tells him she isn't too happy about having to pick up dead chickens. Not by a damn sight, Milton thinks as his anger at the Rodgers sweeps over him again. The Rodgers moved in from New Jersey three years ago and set up as farmers across the road from his place. They've hung a slate sign at their mailbox that says in old English letters "Woodbine."

Real farms have names, but they aren't stuck on signs on the road. Milton's place is known as "Walnut Hill," but there's no sign telling people what they should or do know. Because he is ill, Milton's fury is only rolling at a slow boil. He wants to teach the Rodgers what real farmers are like, or punish them for not being real, but it will be hard since he's too weak to drive his pick-up more than five miles. Over to their chicken houses is two miles, so he ought to make it.

He may be wasting his energies on people who don't mind disasters. When the wind blew the roof off the Rodgers' new pre-fab machine shed, they just ordered a new one. They're experts at getting federal money for disasters. Milton had thought that the governor had to visit by helicopter and declare a whole county a disaster area. He didn't know individuals could get money. For all he knows, the Rodgers claim to be a county instead of a family. They're putting in a swimming pool for Holly Ann, but probably Medicare will pay for it because some one of them says he has a bad back. Hugh Rodgers is a dermatologist who rakes in money from sad kids with pimples and old people with skin cancer. It's clear that Dr. Rodgers knows all the ways to get medical payoffs and tax write-offs. After the Rodgers girl leaves, Milton goes to his day bed to rest and flips the channels for reruns of "Hogan's Heroes." He likes war comedies because they have so much high-spirited destruction and they may give him some good ideas for handling the Rodgers.

He pays a woman to stay with him at home so he doesn't have to go to the hospital to die. She tells her family he is real easy to take care of and entertains himself. It's true. When he's not looking at his programs on the television, he's tuned in to his past where he is the hero and often the only character. Vanity has replaced strength, and he enjoys his starring roles. The old, sick man provides the commentary. "You didn't know you'd be sorry you did that, now did you?" he says to his former strong self-driving the tractor too close to the marsh spreading out from the creek. From the sound of the heavy tractor trailer across the road Milton knows that the Rodgers are getting in a load of baby chickens. Just this year, they have become chicken farmers who think nothing of losing a hundred and fifty "birds," they call the chickens, a night. Until Holly Ann told him, he didn't know they put her to work picking up the dead ones and de-beaking. Next year she'll get to vaccinate she says. It's not right to farm that way or raise a daughter like that. The

Rodgers do things big and wrong—fifty or more thousand chickens, hydroponic greenhouses made out of sheets of polyurethane where the lettuce and tomatoes never touch dirt. They're thinking of pig parlors next, where the pigs live in wooden crates in stacks and never touch the ground. Before the chickens, it was veal barns filled with calves that never tasted anything but a milk formula. It's never-never farming and everyone but Milton thinks it's great. He'd like to burn the whole place down except he knows they have a big fire insurance policy. One chicken house will satisfy him even if it doesn't teach them a lesson.

Every morning he hears the Rodgers hauling away the dead birds, which have smothered when they crowded at the feeders, unable to peck each other out of the way. In cold weather, it's not unusual, he learned from Holly, for five hundred chickens to smother trying to keep warm. Now he can picture Holly Ann in jeans and boots throwing the birds into the truck. The Rodgers don't burn or bury the dead, they spread them over their fields. From the smell carried on the wind, Milton had known a lot of something was dead. Holly Ann said it was better than fertilizer, cheaper.

When Milton had twenty chickens, he knew them by name, heated corn for them in the winter, and buried the old ones he didn't kill for baking hens. He kept his cows like pets. One of his pigs had a rug on the porch and could drink Coke from a bottle.

In Milton's mind, the Rodgers are crazy and mean, but in the county they are called progressive. When they imported some Charolais cows from out west, and tried to feed them mixed chicken manure, straw and molasses, the community watched the white cows almost starve. There was some talk of calling in the Cruelty to Animals people, but they only knew about pets and race horses.

Chickens are animals too, Milton thinks, as he listens to the truck. He knows he's headed down hill fast when he starts sympathizing with chickens. Being ill gives him a lower level of sympathies. He's sorry for the chickens dying in a bank of feathers and heat, but he envies them for being at home when it happened. Huddled up with their friends, or at least their kind, is not the worst way to go either.

Margaret had died at the hospital although her last sensible words to him had been "Let's go home." Bringing her home was the least he could have done. After Margaret's trips to get treatment, she went from being swollen and bald to simian and red-haired. He promised himself at her grave where he had gone especially to make the promise, that he'd take his cancer straight and at home.

A person needs a practice run with death to do it right. But it's too much trouble to refuse the chemo treatments and the final week in the hospital, so he has traded taking the chemo treatments for being able to stay at home to die. It was a trade off with his doctors. The more he thinks about the Rodgers' chickens the more he envies them. They are luckier than people. At least some of them get to die and be picked up at home.

Milton got the youngest doctor to sign a paper saying "the above" should be allowed to stay at home at the end, and although he knows the signature is probably not worth the paper it's written on. Who is at home who would take care of him just to help him take longer to die?

The answer "Nobody" gives him a strange, cheerful freedom. He has a dead son and wife, not to mention the people who should be dead like his uncles. But Margaret is the only one who gave him a practice run with caring for the dying.

His son, Martin, died instantly in a car wreck, a death that was almost not dying, Milton thinks, compared to what Margaret went through to get to the same place. When old people died slowly in the family, all Milton did was visit, send flowers and talk on the telephone and saying families. When Martin was killed, there was nothing to do but the easy things, the arrangements. The dying was over.

Memories of all the funerals he's been to come to him like TV shows, not painful, and in the neon orange and greens of the first color set he and Margaret owned.

Taking chemotherapy and going along with what the doctors say are wearing him out. To keep up a private sense of himself, of his health, as the doctors who know the truth lie to him, is worse than the nausea that attacks at night. He hoards his reserves by simply nodding and saying, "Doing fine." The hard thing is that not all the doctors lie. Some of the young ones believe in telling him the truth—everything. They look as tired as Milton and don't have patience left for niceties, he guesses. The tiredest-looking one signed the paper, shrugging.

The shrug is like the answer "Nobody" to the question, who would take care of him if he lasts longer than October, the month he has picked to die. "Nobody" and the doctor's shrug give him the same jolt that passes for fun.

He remembers the story of the old blind cyclops yelling to his cyclops cousins for help, "Nobody has hurt me! Nobody has hurt me!" Naturally, nobody came to help him. As a boy, he'd thought it was a stupid story, the kind teachers enjoyed, but now he smiles at himself, at the old cyclops yelling "Nobody." One of his teachers used to tell the story of the cyclops and get such a kick out of it, he'd laugh like a fool every time with the kids sitting there bored to death. Now Milton sees the joke.

Maybe he can be the Nobody who starts the fire and clears one chicken house off the face of the earth. There is a lot to be done to plan the fire because the cancer is hitting him faster than he thought it would, even though it runs swiftly in his family. The women in his family are all dead with it. At fifty, he had been sure he had long years left.

The farm market reports steady him. He hasn't been asleep two hours at the most when they come on. Red winter wheat is down, yellow corn up, cows are slightly down this week.

It's June now. The hay is on the ground, and the early garden of spinach, peas and real dirt-touching lettuce has come and gone. The yellow June apples are falling, those the crows left hanging pecked hollow. The cows stand waiting for their treats, not looking up in the branches, just sure of the muffled thuds of the mealy apples to come.

From the swollen intensity in his neck and shoulder as if he had drunk whiskey that concentrated its power just in those two places, he knows he'll be lucky to be here in October.

People have stopped coming to see Milton except the new woman preacher who wants him to call her Tina. It's a little early for the visits to stop. He doesn't count Holly Ann or her mother. He knows he's a project for both of them. He still has his hair and hasn't swelled up yet, and he is still strong enough to finish the hay if he hires two men and all he does is drive the tractor. He can kill the black snake that messes up the pump's water gauge by sleeping on it.

"I'm going, but I'm not gone," he says to Tina, but it's a little too strong for her to take even though she jogs, he heard somewhere.

Sudden death is more suited to neighborhoods. This is how Milton tries to explain to Tina why he's so mad. He asks her if she thinks that's why people love war—it does away with long illness, slow deaths, but she is nervous, looking at the big knuckle of his Adam's apple working and starts talking about her background as a counselor at a veterans' hospital where there was a "great deal of slow dying" from war. He tells her he likes "Mash" and "Hogan's Heroes" better than visits from anyone. He can see a look come on her face that changes his name from Milton Parker to Nobody.

From his experience with Margaret and Hal, Milton knows that neighbors are worse about slow than they are about sudden death. They are impatient for the event, bored with illnesses that go on too long. For an unexpected death though, they go into action in a big way, filling the drive with cars, the house with food, the church with flowers. Milton does not blame human nature. He is the same. He wants to set a fire as much for his sake, to help kill him, as to make a point about how to raise chickens or run a farm. Mrs. Rodgers has tried to be nice, he admits, but she's like a forty-year-old Holly Ann, more interested in herself than in anything he has to offer, except his listening services. The green frozen salad with cherries and coconut put in the fluted cupcake papers she brings him "to tempt his appetite" melt without her noticing even though she cleans it up. She comes in the late afternoon.

"I need the names of some overweight people, some heavies, Mr. Parker," she laughs. "You know I'm the new representative for the Pro-Tek liquid diet here, but we really don't know all that many people, though the ones I've seen could use the Pro-Tek plan. You sure don't need it, so rest easy, I won't be bugging you to death trying to sign you on as a Pro-Tek lifer."

Milton feels his shoulder and neck swell like the cobras he's seen on nature shows.

"If I lose thirty-seven pounds by Christmas, I win a trip to Hawaii, the national headquarters, for Holly Ann and me, plus, I get a life-time supply of Pro-Tek. They sure take care of their own. I'd take all of us to Hawaii if we had anyone to leave in charge of Woodbine while we were away, but there's nobody we can trust. Do you know what I mean? All we need is someone to keep an eye on the place."

The only companionable breeze he feels during the visit is when he hears his word, "Nobody."

"Well, I'd be glad, real glad to watch your place for you, Mrs. Rodgers. Nobody'd do a better job than me." He thinks of himself now not only as an arsonist, but a liar. He feels like somebody again. "A trip would do your family a lot of good. Never been to Hawaii, myself, but I've been on the interstate as far as Tennessee. It did me good to see how bad they build roads now. I mean the farmland they tore up to put those four lanes through burned me up. I came home on the back roads, the ones you can drop letters in the mailboxes from, the curves are so sharp and the shoulders so narrow. I've done all the travelling I want, but like I said, I'd be more than glad to watch out for your place while you all take off."

Milton exhausts himself talking, but the lie is worth it and who knows, he may stretch himself to Christmas and be able to burn him a chicken house in peace. Miracles do happen, as Tina is saying when she leaves. After the fire, he could call long-distance to Hawaii and tell them the bad news.

Mrs. Rodgers wipes up the wet green cupcake paper and the plastic spoon she had brought with her and asks Milton where to throw it. She has a trash compactor and says he needs one. It is clear and comforting to him that she has just offered Woodbine to an arsonist.

Late at night, more war comedies and detective shows, almost as good, come on. Watching them, Milton is full of plans. He'll just set the fire and watch it burn at Christmas. He hopes.

His hopes had been pinned on ruining his heart by moving the hay. The eighty-pound rectangle bales he used to lift would have delivered him to Margaret and their son in a hurry, not that he expects to see them. There'd be too much to say to them that he is not equipped to say. Margaret wouldn't like the fire he is planning, and he's not sure about Martin.

But these new hay rolls as big as Volkswagens that the tractor backs up to and impales on steel needles make exhaustion harder to find, and like chemotherapy keep quick death out of his reach. Before his birthday, next Tuesday, he had wanted to have the hay rolls lined up across the hill.

Mrs. Rodgers' offer for him to keep an eye on Woodbine has saved his life. Now he can live toward Christmas with a little help from the chemo. If he feels he's going back too fast, he'll set the fire earlier, maybe August. Like children who watch television to learn how to commit crimes, he will watch his war comedies more closely to find a scheme to blow up the lettuce and chicken houses, one that will crack his heart open. Two birds with one stone. He grins at his joke. But a fire in December would be better. Meantime, he hopes Mrs. Rodgers drinks her canned drink and loses the prize winning number of pounds. If she does, and if the treatments can get him to Christmas, he won't have to rush in the heat of August to let all the chickens die at home instead of going for fryers. At his leisure in the quiet cold, he can set his fire and add some real dirt to the pipeline of hydroponic juice that would shock the lettuce and tomatoes to death. Smiling, he turns on the radio to catch the end of the evening market report. Milton listens for a minute and then returns to his schemes of arson and how he will stay alive until December. The wily and resourceful Colonel Hogan can serve as his guide. Caught up in his dream of mayhem, Milton's mind floats across the road to the hated chicken houses, while the flat voice of Ed Yancey

200

drones on unheard. "Veal calves up two cents a pound...slaughtered lambs were steady...."

About the Author

Susan Pepper Robbins lives in rural Virginia where she grew up. Her first novel was published when she was fifty ("One Way Home," Random House, 1993). Her fiction has won prizes (the Deep South Prize, the Virginia Prize) and has been published in journals. Her collection of stories "Nothing But the Weather" was published by the indie press Unsolicited Press, and her second novel, "There Is Nothing Strange," was published in England in 2016,. A second collection of stories will be published in 2019. "Local Speed," a novel, came out in 2018 from Unsolicited Press. Her stories focus on the drama of ordinary lives. She teaches writing at Hampden-Sydney College and wrote a dissertation on Jane Austen at the University of Virginia.

About the Press

Unsolicited Press was founded in 2012 and is based in Portland, Oregon. The small press publishes fiction, poetry, and creative nonfiction written by award-winning and emerging authors.

Learn more at www.unsolicitedpress.com